THE Princess AND THE Page

CHRISTINA FARLEY

THE Princess AND THE page

SCHOLASTIC INC.

Library of Congress Cataloging-in-Publication Data available

ISBN 978-1-338-18120-3

10 9 8 7 6 5 4 3 2 1   17 18 19 20 21

Printed in the U.S.A.   40

First printing 2017

Book design by Carol Ly

For Julianne—
muse, fellow princess,
but most importantly,
my sister

Florida

Sleuthing 101: Walk on the balls of your feet.
Bare feet are best for silence and speed.

WEDNESDAY (MERCREDI) JANUARY 15TH

None of this would have happened if Mom had just made macaroni and cheese for dinner. After all, it's got grain and cheese in it. That's two of the five food groups! But no, Mom went on this health kick ever since Dad's doctor told him he had to watch his blood pressure.

"It's time this family got healthy," Mom announced, taking the saltshaker from Dad's hand. "No more eating fast food and frozen dinners."

And that's how it began. The crazy grocery lists, the printed recipes scattered about the kitchen, and her cooking—or should I say burning?—exotic dinners. After last night's near fire fiasco, Mom decided, to our relief, to order our dinners from Healthy Meals Delivered.

"It's the perfect solution," Mom said.

Dad and I agreed.

But tonight as I stare at the dinner menu, I'm thinking charcoaled chicken might not be so horrific.

"This looks great!" Dad kisses Mom on the cheek before filling in the time he arrived home from work on the Lists and Charts Wall. Last year, Mom bought a wall-size whiteboard that she dedicated to keep track of everything we do. When I asked her why, she said it relaxed her.

It's annoying how Dad always goes along with Mom's crazy schemes. Like the charts and graphs and endless nonsense lists and rules. And especially the No Writing Stories rule because apparently stories are a waste of time. Or the craziest one, No Pens in the House rule. Who on this planet has rules like those?

No one. (Oh, wait, no one except *my* family.)

The doorbell rings. Healthy Meals Delivered delivering right on time. I march to the front door, not caring that I'm tromping through the house in my soccer cleats, and fling it open.

A large man wearing all black and holding two square boxes fills the doorway. A green baseball cap covers most of his brown curly hair, and the bill is pulled down so low I've no idea how he can even see.

"Good evening," he says in a gravelly voice. "I have a meal for the Harding family from Healthy Meals Delivered."

"Thanks." I take the boxes.

I push to shut the door, but his boot blocks the path. The man peers past me, assessing the house. I frown, now able to see the man's face clearly. A jagged scar runs from the corner of his eye across to his ear. A trail of chills courses down my back. There's something off about this guy.

"Your foot is in the way," I point out.

"Ah, so it is." He chuckles and then pulls it free from the doorframe. "Enjoy your food. And sweet dreams."

Sweet dreams? What a weirdo. I secure the lock and head to the kitchen. Dad opens the boxes while Mom goes through her list, double-checking the order. After she proclaims the meal satisfactory, we sit down to eat.

But I can't.

"There are green balls on my fish." I pick one up with the edge of my fork.

"Don't be silly, Keira." Mom says, nibbling on something that resembles a weed. "That's a caper. They're delicious."

Visions of creamy macaroni and cheese dance about in my head, causing my stomach to growl. I decide to make the best of this moment and practice my sleuthing skills. While Dad shows Mom his latest data-crunching report, I covertly slip the slimy tomatoes into my napkin and shove them under the edge of my plate.

I'm flicking my capers one by one over my shoulder as inconspicuously as possible, when Dad's fork and knife clatter to the table. His shoulders droop, and then he tumbles off his chair, crashing in a heap on the floor. Mom screams. She bends down, reaching for him, but then she, too, collapses, dropping at his side.

"What are you guys doing?" I say, completely mystified. "Is this a new game or something?"

They don't answer. I set down my fork and peer under the table. They both are so still. As if they were passed out. Or dead.

"Dad! Mom!" I jump out of my chair and dive under the table.

I kneel and grab Mom's hand, searching for a pulse. My breath catches in my throat and it's hard even to breathe, let alone concentrate on what to do next. My ears ring as I press my fingers to Mom's wrist to find a pulse. That's what they trained us to do in PE class. But I can't find her pulse. Every fiber of my being flies into a numbing panic.

Until Dad starts snoring. I pause, confused, and stare at

him. His chest rises and falls. Suddenly, my throat opens up and I'm able to breathe. Beneath my fingers, the gentle thump of Mom's pulse throbs, telling me she's going to be all right. A slight smile curls on her lips and her long blond hair lies about her as if she's pretending to be Sleeping Beauty and having the most wonderful dream.

"You're sleeping?" I say in a choked voice.

I shake Dad and yell in his ear, trying to wake him, but he continues to snore. What is going on? I don't understand why they're sleeping. I lie on the cold linoleum floor between them, burying my face in my hands, my mind whirling.

The front door squeaks. Footsteps clomp through the living room toward the kitchen. Someone is sneaking through our house! My eyes flutter open and I clutch Mom's hand so tightly it nearly turns ashen. I don't move. Through the kitchen chair legs, two sets of boots appear at the kitchen's entrance. My eyes trace up the figures. The boots belong to two men, both dressed in black, one wearing a green baseball cap. My chest stutters and I clamp my eyes shut. I should run, hide, but it's as if my body has forgotten how to move.

"They're out cold," one of the men says in a thick accent I don't recognize. Then he says something in another language to the watch on his wrist. "Let's move. We've got ten minutes max."

The boots tromp back into the living room. I quietly dig through Dad's pockets in hopes of discovering his phone. It's not there. He must have left it on his dresser to charge.

The men begin opening drawers, rifling through them. Papers flutter through the air. Pillows are slashed and feathers scatter about like snow. Picture frames are torn to splinters and lamps are shattered across the ground.

I lick my lips and focus on Rule #12 for sleuthing: "Walk on the balls of your feet. Bare feet are best for silence and speed."

I stealthily slip off my cleats and socks, easing them to the floor. Then, ever so slowly, I creep to the far side of the kitchen, my legs threatening to buckle beneath me. The linoleum bites cold against my feet. With my back pressed against the far wall, I rack my mind, trying to figure out where my parents' phones would be. They got rid of the landline years ago to save money.

Should I go upstairs to find Dad's phone? Mom would tell me to hide. Dad would say run to the neighbors' house.

"Hey!" one of the men says. "The kid isn't lying on the floor anymore."

My heart dives as he steps into the kitchen. The counters are barren, sparkling clean. Not a weapon within my grasp. I slide toward the kitchen's other exit into the hall, when my foot hits something smooth. My soccer ball. I pick it up and kick it as hard as I can at the man's face. My aim is true. It smashes the guy so hard, he slams backward into the wall. With a wail, he slumps to the floor, holding his face.

I spring past him, through the living room and into the hall, sprinting for the front door. There at the other end of the hall, blocking the front door, stands Baseball Cap Guy. His lips curl into a devious grin. I skid to an abrupt stop.

"Having a bad dream, are you?" he says.

I backpedal, only to discover the other man now fills the doorway to the living room I just exited.

"Easy now, little girl." He holds up his hands as if to calm me, but my eyes are riveted to the glowing watch on his wrist. "We don't want to hurt you. If you'll just tell me where your family keeps their *special* things, then everything will be okay."

I clench my fists. As if I'm telling him anything.

I bound up the stairs and sprint down the hall, pumping my arms and focusing on the door at the end. My parents' room. The walls press in too tight. The house suddenly feels too small. I careen inside the room and slam the door shut, clicking the lock. Quickly, I drag Mom's desk chair over and jam it under the doorknob.

The lights flicker. And I'm plunged into darkness. They cut off our electricity.

One of the men pounds on the door, screaming at me to open it. The door shudders. I swallow the lump in my throat, trembling as the wood bulges under the man's bulk.

Don't panic, I tell myself. *Stay strong.*

With only the moonlight to guide me, I rush to Dad's dresser, shoving everything on it to the floor in my search. Wristwatch, comb, magazines, envelopes. It's not here. Then I move to Mom's desk. No phone there either.

The sound of wood splintering cuts deeper into my terror. The chair holding the door scrapes the wooden floor as the door jostles it about. It won't be long before the men will burst in.

A blue glow from the partly open bottom drawer of Dad's dresser captures my attention. Could that be Dad's phone calling? I dive across the room, flinging open the drawer. Shimmering blue light emanates from a long, slim velvet box buried along with Dad's bird books, broken cameras, and shell collection.

A desperate need to open the box overwhelms me. I know I shouldn't waste my time and instead keep searching for the phone.

But I can't.

My hands tremble as I pick up the box. An emblem is imprinted on the top. Two *W*s—one gold, one silver—woven together. Slowly, I open the lid. Glittery blue light showers me and I'm drenched in a cool mist. Tucked within the velvety folds lies an old-fashioned silver pen. Just the sight of it sends a thrill through me. As if I've been waiting my entire life to see it. To touch it.

My fingers curl around its cool surface. It sinks into the center of my palm, feeling as though it was crafted just for my hand. The world washes in blue. Stars swirl around me. Time stops.

It's just me and the pen. My world is complete and I've never felt more alive.

And yet, in the corner of my mind, something nags at me. Something is wrong. Very wrong. Then I remember. There are intruders, terrible men, out to hurt me. I must stop them, but I don't know how.

A stream of ideas bubbles through my head and I *need* to write them down. I snatch up the copy of Dad's *Field and Stream* and, clutching the pen tighter, I scribble out a list on the back flap.

When I finish, the sapphire winds churn in a stream of stars and whispers around me before sinking back into the pen. The room is black once again and the pen is just an antique from Dad's drawer. I drop the magazine from my hand, blinking in confusion. Did I just have a hallucination? I've heard that kind of stuff happens when people undergo massive stress.

"Open this door right now!" the man yells, pulling me back to the moment. "Or I'll hurt your parents. Then they won't be having such lovely dreams anymore, will they?"

Those words spur me to action. I stare at my list on the back of the magazine lying on the floor. What if this list actually worked? I rush to the bed where Dad's suit jacket is laying, just where the list said it would be. Then I dig into the pocket and discover his phone. Just like the list said.

I dial 911 and quickly explain the situation to the operator. Relief floods me when she tells me the police will be here within minutes.

But my relief is short-lived as the door splinters along the center and the hinges bend one by one. I clutch Dad's phone tighter. I have only seconds before the door comes crashing down. Frantically, I continue down my list.

I rip up the loose floorboard by the bedroom door, which creates a good-sized hole. Mom always complained to Dad to fix it, but now I'm glad he was too busy. Next I sprint into their bathroom, grab the bottle of shampoo, and step back out to dump it on the floor outside the bathroom door. I pause, panting. What is next on the list? The hinges of the bedroom door groan.

Shells! I run over and grab a handful of them from Dad's dresser drawer and toss them onto the shampoo just as the bedroom door begins to snap off a hinge. I snatch up the lamp from the bedside table as my final weapon of self-defense and hide behind the curtains just as the door crashes open against the bedroom wall.

"It's gotta be in here," one of them says. "She must know about it."

I peek from behind the curtain. Flashlight beams slice the darkness. The men barrel into the room, but one steps into the hole, which swallows up his entire leg, and he starts screaming in agony. Ignoring his buddy, Baseball Cap Guy heads toward the bathroom but slips on the shampoo, his legs skidding across the floor like losing control on an ice rink. He falls into a heap, groaning. Outside, sirens cut through the intruders' shouting.

"The cops are here!" Stuck Guy says.

Baseball Cap Guy crawls across the wooden floor, picking off the shells stuck to him. But then he pauses and his flashlight lands on the opened copy of *Field and Stream*. My list! He picks it up, reading over my words as he rises to his feet. My hands grow cold when his head swivels to where I'm hiding, peeking out from behind the curtain. He knows I'll be there because it's number five on the list.

"Help me up, man!" Stuck Guy says. "My foot is stuck and the police will be here any second."

But Baseball Cap Guy just leers in my direction. He rips off the back cover of *Field and Stream* where my list is and tucks it into his pocket. Then he turns and vanishes into the hallway.

I sag to the floor as police swarm into the room and arrest the intruder who's stuck in the hole. Someone turns the lights on and a paramedic rushes over to check me for injuries. I refuse to move, sitting there in a daze, clutching the lamp, until my parents stumble in shortly afterward, now awake and complete wrecks. I should feel safe now that they are all here to protect me.

But I don't.

"Oh, Keira!" Mom says, wrenching the lamp from my grasp as Dad talks to the police about the burglary. "Are you okay? I can't believe I fell asleep while you were all alone with those horrible men."

"I'm fine," I lie.

She helps me up and directs me to the bed. Its soft cover soothes my nerves. Suddenly, though, Mom releases me, her eyes and mouth widening as she sees something from the other side of the room. As if in a trance, she staggers to Dad's opened drawer and lifts up the empty velvet box.

"They took the pen!" Her voice quivers as she shows Dad and the officer.

"Oh no," Dad murmurs, and he wraps his arms around Mom.

"Is there a problem, ma'am?" the officer asks. "Is it a special pen? An heirloom?"

"They took it!" She shakes the box in the officer's face. "This is what they came here for!"

The officer nods, but his expression remains quizzical as he notes Mom's complaint. "They stole a pen, you said? Could you explain it to me? Is there anything else you noticed they stole?"

This is the moment when I should run up to Mom and give her the pen. Show her I found it and then everything will be okay. I reach into my pocket to take it out, but as my fingers touch its cool surface, it tickles my skin and I remember that rush of power I felt as I wrote the list.

I can't give it up.

Ever.

2

*Fact: Both Cinderella and Snow White
have wicked stepmothers.*

I tug on the hem of my practice jersey as I pause at the top
of the stairs. Memories from last night throb at the back of
my mind as I survey the stark living room. While I slept in,
Mom and Dad must have cleaned up the mess. The walls
are barren. The cushions have disappeared from the couches,
and the broken glass is gone. I swallow the lump in my
throat and head toward the smell of something burning in the
kitchen.

A glance at the counter reveals the source of the smell—a
plate stacked with burnt toast.

In the center of the room, Mom is cramming papers into a
trash can. Labels that once had been placed carefully all around
the house are now strewn at her feet.

"Keira!" Mom abandons her pile to grab my shoulders,
her blue eyes stare intently at me. "How did you sleep? Are
you okay?"

"I guess. What are you doing?"

"Cleaning." She wipes the sweat off her forehead and goes
back to jamming the rest of the papers into the trash can. Her
hair is tied up in a blue ribbon and she's wearing her Soccer
Mom T-shirt. The one with the big O on it that looks like a
soccer ball. After she explains how the police arrested the

burglar, and Dad is out getting a new security system, she scoops a handful of pencils from one of the drawers and chucks them on top of the discarded papers.

"You're throwing pencils away?" I peer into the trash can. It's brimming with paper and pencils. I pick out the soccer ball pencil I bought at Chadwicks Stationery. Mom snatches it from my hand and tosses it back into the trash.

"After last night, we need to refocus our priorities," she says. "We can't take any more risks. It's best if we got rid of *all* writing utensils and papers. We can't be too careful."

"You think the robbery was because of the missing pen?"

"That old thing?" Mom tosses the electronic pencil sharpener into the trash can. "No. It was my mother's and I was just feeling overly sensitive about it last night."

Guilt tugs at me. After the police left, I stashed the pen in my secret writing compartment. Maybe I should give it back to Mom. Maybe then she wouldn't freak out so bad. But when she starts ripping the lists and charts off the kitchen wall, anger rolls inside me.

Why does she have to overreact and control everything in my life? This is way worse than when I got the sports editor job at school and she flipped out. I managed to keep that job only because I convinced her I wouldn't be writing fiction. Writing anything imaginary is strictly prohibited in my family. It's practically the family religion. Facts, data, charts: These keep the world spinning. Fiction is for freaks.

Harding Family Rule #1: Do not write fiction.

Harding Family Rule #2: No pens allowed.

But this morning, she's finally gone wacko and it looks like nonfiction and pencils are off-limits now, too. I cross my arms, holding back the storm inside me. If the pen is just an "old thing," then she won't miss it.

"How am I supposed to do my homework without paper and pencils?"

"We'll figure something out. Don't you worry." But her smile doesn't reach her eyes. They're cloudy blue this morning. The color of the sky when a rain shower settles in for a long haul. "I made you some toast. It's whole wheat with hummus. Super healthy."

I shuffle to the counter and the plate of burnt toast. A white spread covers the top. I nibble at the corner only to spit it out. The white stuff isn't hummus or even butter. The jar of mayonnaise beside the plate has got to be the culprit. *Gross.*

The doorbell rings. Mom and I freeze.

"I'll get it," she says all nonchalantly, but her body stiffens as she picks up her cell phone and heads for the door.

"I'll be your backup." I flash a smile and grab my soccer ball.

It's Bella, my best friend since second grade, standing there wearing a purple polka-dotted shirt that makes her black curls shine. She smiles widely as Mom welcomes her inside. Since she lives only three houses down the street, we hang out often, especially at the park because I rarely invite her to my house. The last time she went into my kitchen, she asked a hundred questions about Mom's lists and graphs. It was completely mortifying. But then, Bella's house is always brimming with material and sewing machines for her mom's fashion business that she recently launched, so there's never room there for us to hang out either.

"Hey, Bells!" I say, and wave for her to come in. I try to block out the thought that Baseball Cap Guy stood right in this spot less than twenty-four hours ago. "What are you up to?"

"I heard about last night," she says as Mom leaves us to continue her cleaning escapades. "That's so horrible. Are you okay?" I shrug. "Well, don't worry. I'm here to cheer you up and get your mind off it all. Mom is having one of her big designer parties at the house, so I thought your house would be the perfect place to escape."

"Sure," I say. "Come on up."

⋆   ⋆   ⋆

"You want me to do what?" I flip through the magazine Bella brought.

"It's not a big deal." Bella plops down on my bed, staring at me with those big puppy dog eyes of hers. "Fairy tales are easy to write, aren't they? Plus, maybe it'll help get your mind off everything after last night."

I'm not sure anything will get my mind off last night or that look Baseball Cap Guy flashed before he escaped the police. "I don't know," I say. "How do we even know it's not some kind of scam?"

"It's *Girls' World*!" Bella sticks the magazine in my face. "If they aren't legit, then who is?"

I suppress a smile. "Point taken."

"*Don't* give me that look."

Bella may be my best friend, but she veers toward the gullible side. "Come on." I roll my eyes. "It's a magazine that tells you what to wear and how to bake cupcakes."

"Don't bash the cupcakes!" Then she flips to page 16. "Just read it."

A silhouette of a princess set against an outline of a castle fills the magazine page. *Fairy Tales Do Come True* swirls in flowing script across the top.

Win a Fairy Tale!

Win a fairy-tale vacation to a French castle in the famous Loire Valley. Entrants must be between 8 and 12 years of age. Winner receives a trip for four to France, airfare included, to become a princess for one week in a fairy-tale castle. On the final night, a ball will be held in the winner's honor, including her own ball gown to keep.

To enter, write a 2,000-word fairy tale. Fill in the form
below and attach it to your story.

"It is pretty dreamy." I totally can imagine myself flying off to France with Bella. I skim the rest of the advertisement, which explains where to send the story, and the deadline. "You're right. It does look legit. But you really want me to enter? Me, the skeptic. Me, the hater of all things pink? And besides, the deadline is like tomorrow!"

"For my entire life, I've dreamed of visiting a castle and living the life of a princess. And here is our chance sitting right in front of us." Bella tilts her head as she puckers her lower lip. "I was thinking if we both enter, we'll increase our chances of winning, right?"

"Increases them from none to slim." I tuck my flannel pillow against my stomach. "So let's just say that I wrote this amazing fairy tale—even though they make me feel like I'm going to puke fried bananas—I'd still have to enter the contest. And you know how my parents feel about me writing stories."

"Then don't tell them. It'll be our secret."

"Trust me, that's so tempting." I sigh and shake my head. "But if I won? Mom would totally flip. I'd be grounded for an eternity."

"Don't you think it's strange your parents don't allow you to write stories? I mean, you're twelve years old!"

If she only knew. "Mom says I should spend more time on my math and science. Subjects that deal with reality and truth will help me get a better job."

Bella stares at me as if I'm a pink-headed unicorn. I wonder if Bella would still be my friend if she knew the extent of my family's rules or saw my mom downstairs throwing away perfectly good writing materials. My life is crazy enough as it is and the last thing I want is to lose Bella's friendship. Besides, right now Mom is downstairs stripping more of my freedom away with every new idea she has. Maybe I need to keep something for myself.

I toss my pillow aside and head to a corner of the room. With the edge of a penny, I pry out the loose piece of baseboard, revealing a hole where my secret writing stash is located.

"What *are* you doing?" Bella says.

"Getting my supplies." My journal, favorite pencil, a stack of papers, and Twizzlers are right where I left them. I lightly touch my new pen. A spark of blue bursts from its surface as if it's winking at me. But I leave it hidden. Safe.

"You hide your supplies? That's so weird."

The memory of when this whole madness began still haunts me. I was six years old, lying on the living room floor and writing about a picture I'd drawn of a girl with Pegasus. Mom spotted the Pegasus and gasped. She ripped the story from me, tearing it into tiny shreds, and then began frantically peeking out the windows as if she was afraid someone had seen me. I started crying.

"There now." Mom pulled me into a hug. "We know you are going to be incredibly successful someday. But in order for that to happen, don't write any more stories. It's the math and science, the hard facts, that are going to bring you success. I know other people imagine stuff, but in our family, we focus on what is real and true."

My face burns at the memory.

"It makes writing more fun having secret compartments," I say breezily. "Don't you think?"

"Oh!" Bella practically bounces on the bed. "Then you're going to enter the contest?"

"Don't get too excited." I bite off the end of a Twizzler strip and hand the bag to her. I try to focus on my journal rather than the blue tinge emanating from the baseboard where the pen is hidden away. I position myself on the bed so that I block Bella's view from the glow.

"All right. But you've got to help me. First: The princess needs a name," I begin.

"How about Gabrielle?" Bella suggests. "That sounds princessy and French."

"Perfect." I chomp another bite. "Something needs to go wrong, but do princesses even have problems?"

"Well." She looks up from her story, chewing on the bottom of her lip. "There's Sleeping Beauty who got on the bad side of a fairy and then Snow White had that wretched stepmom."

"I thought that was Cinderella." I rub my forehead. "Ugh. They're all the same!"

"Then I guess you should have a stepsomebody in the story," she says, giggling.

"A stepsister, then." I start writing. "A nasty, wicked stepsister. After all, a fairy tale has to have a bad guy—or girl in this case."

An image of the castle crystallizes in my mind. The sun glistening off stained-glass windows, the shadows from the fading day deepening on the parapet, and a jealous stepsister.

Once upon a time, there lived a princess and her stepsister. The two were inseparable best friends and had everything they ever wanted.

"Don't forget to make sure someone falls in love," Bella adds. "I adore a good romance."

One bright summer day when the forget-me-nots were in bloom, Princess Gabrielle met a lonely prince visiting from a faraway land at her birthday party.

Once I start writing, I can't stop. I write a full page, but then pause.

"The story feels too perfect." I tap my pencil to my lips as I think. "Oh! How about this?" I read my words out loud for Bella.

> *"But the stepsister also fell deeply in love with the prince, and the thought of him loving another was too much for her to endure. If he could not love her, she was determined he would love no one. So she—"*

I groan. "So what *does* she do?"

"Beats me." Bella sighs and rolls onto her back. "I'm getting nowhere real quick, too. What we need is a good luck charm. Or a fairy who would grant us a wish."

I tug on the bottom of my shirt, unable to stop thinking about my pen tucked away safely in its compartment. What would happen if I used it? Would it give my story good luck? Grant my wish?

The door opens. It's Mom carrying a tray of juice and carrot sticks. Her smile vanishes as her eyes pan across our writing materials. I toss my Manchester United throw over my journal, but it's too late. She's already seen the evidence.

Mom calmly, *way* too calmly, sets the tray on the table and clasps her hands in front of her. She smiles, but her eyes are steel, cutting and hard as they bore into me.

"What are you girls doing?" she says.

"Er." Bella side-glances at me, unsure what to say. "We were making a list?"

Any other day, that would've worked for Mom. But not today. Definitely not today.

I plaster on my most innocent face. "Hey, Mom." I pick at the corner of the throw. "We were writing a school report."

"You were *writing*?" She marches to the bed and yanks away the throw. "This doesn't look like a school report." Her fingers trail down the paper as she scans the words. "This is a story!" She wads it up and throws it in the trash can.

"It's not what it seems. It's a fairy tale. That's a form of nonfiction, right?"

Mom's chin lowers and she lifts her eyebrows skeptically.

"For class." Inwardly, I cringe. Okay, I need to stop lying. Things are getting out of hand. "We were asked to write a fairy tale for a contest. It's nothing big."

"Please, Mrs. Harding," Bella says. "I was just trying to cheer her up."

"I guess there isn't any harm in it," Mom says, but I spot that gleam in her eyes. She's just saying that for Bella's sake. "You had good intentions."

Bella's phone beeps. "Oh, broomsticks!" she says. "I've got to go. Mom says she needs help cleaning up after her show. Promise you'll call me if you have any brain blocks."

"I promise," I say, but wince at Mom's glare.

"Au revoir!" Bella says. I give a halfhearted wave, wishing she didn't have to leave.

As soon as the front door slams shut, Mom starts gathering up the papers and writing supplies.

"I can't believe you said all that in front of Bella!" I say. "It was embarrassing!"

"She wasn't robbed last night. She's safe and doesn't understand what we have to deal with."

"You're taking all of my writing supplies, too. That's not fair! You can't do that."

"I can and I will. I'm doing this for your safety."

"No, you're not! You're doing it because you want to control my life. You don't care what I want or what I like to do."

"Now, don't overreact." Mom's shoulders sag. "Maybe it's

time to get you a computer. It will be such a relief when you're out of school and don't have any of these reports to do. You'll get a nice job where you won't have to write."

"But why?" I clench my fists. My face burns like it's on fire. "What's wrong with writing? There could be worse things than writing stories. So what if I can't have a successful career as a writer? All these stories are bursting in my head, and I want to write them!"

"Oh, sweetie." Mom bites her lip, tears crowding the corners of her eyes. She reaches for me, but I step away, crossing my arms, needing the distance. "When I was a kid, I got myself into a lot of trouble with my words. I did something irresponsible, and I nearly lost everything because of it. I don't want that to happen to you. I'll do anything, *anything*, to keep you safe and let you be who you're truly meant to be."

"Because you made that mistake doesn't mean I should be punished for it!" And just like that, all the anger and frustration over last night stirs up a storm inside me. I point at the trash can, my hand shaking. "Writing stories like this can't hurt anyone and you know it. It's the stupidest thing I've ever heard and I'm sick of it."

"Keira!" Mom takes a deep breath. "You have to trust me on this. I'm looking out for you."

"No, you're not. You just want to control me. Admit it."

"Focusing on things that aren't real, and living in an imaginary world is dangerous." All her sweetness vanishes, replaced by red cheeks. "I'm trying to keep you safe. And if that means I have to be a little controlling, so be it."

With those words, she leaves, her back stiff as a board. I kick my door closed behind her. The walls shudder.

I glare at the door as I dig my hands into my hips. My anger has built into a hurricane that won't stop swirling, whooshing through me, begging to be released. I start kicking my soccer ball against the wall, smashing it hard, kick after kick. Mom hates it when I play soccer in the house, but she doesn't come to stop me, so I know she's madder than mad.

My ball knocks over our family picture on my bedside stand. I pick it up and set it back in its place. It's the three of us with white-toothed smiles, wearing matching khaki pants and blue tops. We look like the perfect family.

But we aren't. Something is wrong with us. Very wrong. I can feel it in the pit of my stomach.

The blue light beams through the cracks of my secret hiding spot calling for me. I bend down and pop open the baseboard. The pen glistens as though it's made of a million sapphires. As I pick it up, blue winds burst out of the pen and rush around me, just like last night, swirling, whirling in a magical madness. Once again, time freezes and words whisper, spinning about like pixies on a warm summer day. My hand aches to finish my fairy tale. That desperate need to pour out my anger and frustration over Mom and her rules overwhelms me.

I rescue the crumpled fairy tale from the trash can and smooth it out. It's time someone wrote a fairy tale that showed real life, where people don't live happily ever after and don't get their way.

The power of my words rumbles through my chest, echoing and clambering for escape.

I know I shouldn't.

But I also know I must. So I release the words, letting them whirl around me and spill across the page. People and new worlds are woven with each stroke of my pen, creating a story of magic and romance.

Then I scrawl out the ending in fierce, hard strokes.

On the night of the ball celebrating the engagement of Princess Gabrielle and the prince, the stepsister swooped

*into the castle amid the celebration. The knights and the
queen tried to stop the stepsister, but failed. In her fury,
the stepsister cast a powerful spell, banishing the queen,
her court, the prince, and Princess Gabrielle to the Dark
Tower, where they would never live happily ever after.
The stepsister now rules the kingdom with force and evil
magic, killing any who steps in her path. No one dares
stand against her.*

THE END

The words glisten on the paper like stars in a midnight sky.

A breeze tasting of salty tears and lilies whips across my
face. The sapphire colors spin around me—once, twice—
before being sucked back into the pen. My room hangs in
silence. The pen becomes simply an old antique, and my words
are merely scrawled in blotted ink.

But deep down inside, I know something happened.

A magic terrifyingly wonderful.

France

Tip of the Day: If a fairy godmother warns you to hurry home by the stroke of midnight, you should listen.

FRIDAY (VENDREDI), JUNE 11TH

"*Voilà*," the driver announces. "Welcome to *Château de Chenonceau, mademoiselles.*"

"What did he say?" Bella riffles through her French language book for the zillionth time.

"I think he said we're here." I yank open the taxi door and step out of the car, gravel crunching beneath my feet.

To think that I actually won the fairy-tale contest blows my mind. But now, standing here in the heart of France, about to stay in a French castle for a week with my best friend and Mom, is beyond anything I could ever have hoped for. I wish Dad could've come, but since he had to work, he told us to think of it as a girls' trip. An escape from the memories of the break-in.

Oak trees branch out like a canopy above and the air smells of flowers. A stone guardhouse stands about ten feet away, next to a massive wrought iron gate. I drag my suitcase behind me as I rush to peer through the bars.

A dirt lane runs as straight as an arrow, racing from my feet through the path to the castle.

Someone clears their throat, jolting the three of us back to reality. It's the gatekeeper, wearing a spotless blue uniform. He has a slight smile on his round, tanned face. Probably because we're standing outside the castle gates, heads back, mouths open like total idiots.

"You must be Margaret and Keira Harding, and Isabella Francois," he says as he checks his clipboard. "From *Girls' World*?"

"Yes," we say.

"May I see your passports?" After he gives them a quick glance, he says, "*Bonjour*. I will open the gate, but please wait. Allow me to call Pierre. He will pick you up. Princesses should never have to walk such a distance." He winks before ducking back inside the miniature house.

"He just called us princesses!" Bella squeals.

"Princesses." I grin. "I could handle that for a week."

"A week?" Bella snorts. "More like a lifetime."

A guy riding a golf cart buzzes out of a side building and veers straight toward us as the gate creaks open. The cart jolts to a stop before us. A tall and lanky man with short black hair leaps out and bows. He's wearing brown pants and a cream-colored button-down shirt that looks well-worn, but neatly pressed.

"*Mademoiselles*, I am Pierre. May I escort you to *le château*?"

"*Oui!*" Bella says, beaming. "Yes, you may."

Pierre loads up our suitcases while we all slide into the cart. We take off, flying down the avenue, wind rushing against my cheeks. We stop at the bridge of the most beautiful castle I could imagine. I gawk in awe at how the castle itself acts as a bridge, stretching over the entire river.

The afternoon sun sparkles on the water below. A blue flag waves in the afternoon breeze from one of the four turrets. The pointed peaks remind me of upside-down ice-cream cones. Along the slanted roof in the front, three intricate windows jut out of dormers. A broad staircase runs up to the bridge, which crosses a moat and leads to the castle's massive double-door entrance. A balcony is just above it on the second floor. The castle glistens like fresh snow, all pure and sparkly.

Château de Chenonceau.

"It's like it's been snipped out of a storybook and slapped here for the world to see," I tell Bella and Mom as we all step out of the cart. "You know what's so cool; it's exactly how I imagined the castle in my fairy tale."

"It's even more beautiful than Cinderella's castle." Bella sighs as she lifts her sunglasses to the top of her head. "It's everything I've dreamed of and more."

"You're right," I whisper. "It is *magical*."

Mom's smile turns into a frown. "Let's hope not. It looks like a perfectly normal building to me. Nothing unusual to it."

"Right," I say, grasping for facts to appease her.

For the past month, Mom and I have made lists of interesting facts about the countryside and the castle. We even got a new calendar on castle facts. Once I got news that I won the contest, I told her I'd typed the story. I don't know why I lied. Maybe because I could totally see Mom canceling the whole trip if she suspected that I used the special pen.

So I quickly spew off a few facts to calm her. "The building of the castle began in 1515," I recite. "And the architecture is a mix of late Gothic and early Renaissance."

Pierre begins to unload the luggage and waves his hand at the entrance.

"I think he means for us to go ahead," Mom says.

Before I even touch the knocker of the large front doors, one of them swings open. A thin man with slicked brown hair, an angular face, and black suit jacket meets me. He dips into a bow, causing his long suit tails to flip up behind him.

He must be the butler, I decide. A butler who looks as if he's off to the opera.

"*Bonjour*," I say, expecting him to say something. He doesn't.

I shrug and step past him into a long cream-colored hall smelling of old wood and lilies. The floor, mahogany-colored tiles, shines brighter than Mom's kitchen floor, which is really saying something. A bright red carpet rests in the center like a wedding runner. Rooms fork off, and the ceiling rises so high a ladder couldn't touch the triangular ribbed arches. Mirrors and life-size paintings hang on the walls, and a round table sits in the center of the hall with fresh-cut lilies in a vase.

"*Bonjour, mademoiselles!*" A woman bustles toward us. She has pale skin that looks like it's been caked with powder, and her black eyes appear almost sunken. Her graying hair is pulled back in a bun so tightly her face appears pinched. "The gatekeeper rang to say you had arrived. I am the housekeeper of the château. So you see, it is my responsibility to make sure everything runs its course properly and efficiently."

A large grandfather clock resting against a wall starts tolling. *Boom. Boom. Boom.* There's something about the sound that sends spider chills down my back. Mom checks her watch when the clock doesn't stop at two.

"Looks like your clock is off," Mom says. "My watch says it's two in the afternoon."

"Ignore the clock," the housekeeper says over the clanging. "It is broken."

I try to smile, but the housekeeper only frowns back. Now that I think about it, this lady could've passed as a witch at Halloween.

"My name is Madame DuPont. You will call me Madame." She smooths down her black jacket and skirt of nonexistent wrinkles. "There. Introductions have been made." I raise my eyebrows. She hadn't even asked for our names. "Come. I will escort you to your chambers."

Once Madame turns her back to lead the way, Bella clutches her neck and starts pretending she's being strangled. I snicker, clamping my hand over my mouth. Madame spins around just in time to see Bella, back arched and tongue dangling out of her mouth. From Madame's scowl and pointed look, it's obvious Madame doesn't appreciate good acting.

"I see I can't wait until we get upstairs to lay out the rules of *le château*," she snaps.

Bella and I jerk to a military stance, which seems the best course of action at a time like this.

"There will be no degrading property, running within these halls, mischief, or stealing." She glares at us—even Mom—as if we're convicted criminals. "If you leave the property, you must be supervised by an adult. Curfew will be at ten p.m. sharp. At which time, you must be in your room, door locked. No sneaking about."

"Curfew?" I say.

Madame glowers. "There will be no arguing about the rules. And finally, remember that the kitchen and attic are restricted."

"We will gladly comply with your rules," Mom says. "It's lovely to have everything so clearly organized and laid out. If you would be so kind, could I have a printout of those?"

Madame ignores my mom, instead giving us a good stare-down with those creepy eyes of hers before continuing her march down the hall.

"Geez," Bella mutters. "Maybe we're at the wrong place. This is sounding more like a dungeon."

"Really?" I whisper to Bella as we head upstairs. "After that list of rules, I'm beginning to feel right at home."

Madame strides down a corridor mirroring the one downstairs, to a front room on the left. Reaching into her pocket, she withdraws a large key ring. It jingles with a mass of old metal keys.

Muttering in French, she selects a thin silver key and slips it into the lock. The wooden door creaks open, but when I enter the room, I instantly decide I love it. It's a corner room with two large windows, one on each outer wall, so that sunshine fills every crevice.

"This was once the bedchamber of Gabrielle d'Estrées," Madame explains. The name *Gabrielle* makes my head snap up. That's the same name as the character in my story! It's as though this room was destined for me! Then Madame clears her throat as if her necklace is clutched too tightly and continues, "But I prefer to simply call it the Corner Room. This will be Keira and Isabella's room."

"It's very sparse," Bella points out. "Very bare. It really could have some decor added."

Tapestries cover the white stone walls. Carved golden-colored beams make up the ceiling, and the floor is tiled. A wide red carpet is positioned under the red brocade canopy bed. I guess with Bella's decorating skills, she might think it's sparse, but I thought it pretty complete with desk, chair, wardrobe, floor lamp, and square table holding a bouquet of lilies. Still, if anyone could make a room gorgeous, it would be Bella. She's got the eye for decorating like no one else.

"This is lovely," I say with a contented sigh, tracing my hand over the desk.

"The owner doesn't like clutter." Madame waves Pierre away once he deposits our luggage by the door. He bows and disappears. "The owner, Monsieur Monteque, is a proponent of order and cleanliness, which I presume you will honor."

As if to prove her point, Madame strides across the room, trails her finger across the desk, and then inspects her fingertip for dust. Apparently, she doesn't find anything out of place since she clasps her hands together and says, "Unpack and freshen up. Mrs. Harding, allow me to show you to your room. It is just across the hall."

Once the two of us are alone, Bella giggles. She lifts her chin and mimics Madame's voice, saying, "A proponent of order and cleanliness."

Laughing, I snatch up a tasseled bed cushion and toss it at Bella. "Okay, stop it already! Only one witch allowed per castle."

"Now, you'll pay for that, my little dearie," Bella sings in her best Wicked Witch of the West voice. She picks up another pillow, and we launch into a pillow fight.

A knock at the door sends the cushions sailing back onto the bed. Red-faced, we snap to attention. A maid peeks her head around the door.

"S'il vous plait," the maid squeaks. "My name is Camille and if you should need anything, do tell me. Tea will be served in the sitting room in thirty minutes. Your mother said she wished to take a rest, so she will not be attending."

"Okay. Merci," I say.

Once the maid disappears, Bella collapses onto the bed, laughing. "This trip is going to be so great."

"I know, right? I can't believe how lucky we are."

Or maybe it isn't luck at all.

I think about the sapphire colors whirling around me in a sparkling dance as I wrote the words of the fairy tale. What was that? Was it magic? Was it my imagination?

Suddenly, the desperate need to hold the pen rages through my core. To touch the pen's smooth surface, to watch the words spin about me like fireworks, to allow the power of it to flow through me as I write.

I dig through my suitcase, frantically tossing my clothes aside until I find the pen where I buried it in one of my socks. A quick glance over my shoulder tells me Bella isn't paying attention, too busy talking to her mom on her phone. I'm not sure why I don't want to show her the pen, but right now I just want to keep it as my own secret.

The pen slips out of the sock and into my palm. It shimmers once, almost as if it's whispering to me. Promising me wonders to come.

I squeeze it tight and press it to my chest, soaking in the magic flowing from it.

4

Ancient Castle Fact: No toilets.
(Unless your idea of a toilet is just a hole in the floor.)

After we unpack and splash water over our faces, we head downstairs and follow the sound of voices in hopes of discovering the sitting room and, more important, food. We find ourselves standing in the doorway of the most glamorous sitting room I've ever seen. With the velvet-covered furniture and gold-trimmed ceiling, it's a room fit even for King Louis XIV himself.

"Oh!" Bella says, and her fingers twitch as she hugs her design sketchbook. I know that sign. She wants to sketch all the decorating ideas she's seeing. "This is a designer's paradise."

I, on the other hand, find the people fascinating. I suppose it's the writer in me. An elderly couple sits on the smaller couch, sipping from teacups. The white-haired lady reminds me of Old Mother Hubbard with all those wrinkles. She takes up more than half the space on the couch due to her size. The man next to her is as skinny as she is large. He leans his head back against the couch, snoring. He has these thick, bushy white eyebrows that quiver with every snore.

As Bella and I stroll into the room, Old Mother Hubbard elbows him. He snorts and jerks like a pecking rooster as he's startled awake.

In the corner, by the fireplace, a long-legged man lounges in a wingback chair. The newspaper in his hands crinkles as he glances up over it. He drops his pointed chin and scrutinizes us above his spectacles with his brown eyes. His black hair is sculpted in a perfect swoop. I bet he spent a lot of time and gel to get that perfect arc. As if bored with what he sees, he hides back behind his newspaper.

Mother Hubbard smiles. "Good day." She pats the bun in her hair and adjusts what looks like knitting needles that apparently hold her bun in place.

"Hi," Bella and I chorus as we settle on the empty flowered couch.

"My name is Rose Jones, and this is my husband, Mr. Jones. We are from England. Somerset, actually," Mother Hubbard says. "My husband and I are here for the week on our second honeymoon."

"Nice to meet you," I say, trying to be civilized. "My name is Keira and this is my best friend, Bella."

A woman waltzes in with a tray holding two teacups and a plate of scones. A giant puffy hat is perched on her head, reminding me of whipped cream. She's a hefty woman who carries her bulk with purpose. Her dark brown hair is twisted back into a low bun, and she has thick eyebrows that form a wall across her face. She sets the tray on a side table and pours us each a steaming cup of tea.

"*Bonjour,*" she says, passing me a cup. "I am zee cook. My English ees not good, but I am learning so I can be an international chef someday."

"*Merci.*" I take a scone from the offered plate and add it to my tea saucer. "That sounds like a wonderful plan."

I sit rigid, praying my tea won't spill all over the embroidered couch, but somehow I manage a tight smile. Oddly, the cook doesn't smile back. In fact, her expression makes me think she just drank soured milk.

"At least you will not die from zee food," the cook says as she places the teapot on the tea server. "Zat much I can promeese."

I choke on my scone and watch in horror as a splash of tea spills on the couch. But the cook doesn't pay any mind; instead, she whizzes out of the room.

"What's that supposed to mean?" I say.

"Wow. She's kind of morbid, isn't she?" Bella says.

"She said that because the castle is haunted," a boy's voice says from above.

Startled, I peer up to see a boy about my age with black spiked hair, wearing a loose-fitting T-shirt and jeans. The T-shirt says EVEREST OR BUST! He's squatting inside a small window alcove above a china cabinet, with a mischievous grin.

"Oh, dear." Mrs. Jones begins fanning herself.

"How did you get up there?" Bella asks.

"Haunted?" I say curiously, setting down my teacup.

"Chet Parker!" the man who had been hiding behind his newspaper yells. "Get down this instant before Madame sees you and kicks us off the premises. We've only been here a day and she's already threatened twice."

Chet scoots to sit on the cabinet's edge, then pushes off the side with his hands. When he launches from the cabinet, his feet first touch the wall before he drops to the floor with the ease of a cat.

"Wow." Bella's eyes are as wide as her scone. "Cool move."

"Well! I never," Mrs. Jones exclaims, holding her hand to her chest. "Do come and sit with us and have yourself a scone straightaway before you give us all a heart attack."

Chet smiles easily and saunters over to plop into a chair. He cocks his head in my direction and says, "Yep. Haunted. Well, not so much during the day. But last night, I could've *sworn* I saw a ghost."

Bella nearly drops her teacup. I snatch it from her hands just in time.

"A ghost?" she whispers. "Here?"

"Now, don't be scaring the girls," Chet's dad says, and then to Bella and me, "Chet has been a tad bored here. Making up all kinds of nonsense to pass the time. Good thing you two arrived. Maybe you can keep him out of trouble."

Chet laughs and shrugs, not denying his dad's words. Still, I can't help but notice how the Joneses don't refute Chet's story of ghosts as they shift uneasily in their chairs, staring at the carpet.

"Right," Chet says. "So as you heard from my dad there, I'm Chet Parker."

Before I can open my mouth to introduce myself, Mrs. Jones jumps in. "This is Keira and Bella. They are from the States."

"The States, huh?" Chet grabs a scone and wolfs it down in one gulp. "We're from Montreal, but my family is originally from China. Are you here on holiday?"

"Keira won a writing contest from a magazine," Bella says. "A fairy tale for four at a French castle. Her mom and I came with her."

"That's cool," Chet says. "I really wanted to go on a rock climbing trip down south, but Dad's kind of obsessed with castles. This one is okay except it's been *really* boring, so it's a good thing you guys showed up before I lost my marbles. I could show you around. Maybe if we're lucky, we'll run into that ghost."

"Just remember rule number one," Mr. Parker tells Chet from behind his paper. "Don't break anything."

* * *

"Did Madame give you guys the rule spiel, too?" Chet asks us as we enter the dining room. An oak table sits in the center with twelve chairs padded in thick red velvet.

"Yeah, something about not degrading the property," I say.

"I'm afraid you can thank me for that rule," Chet says. "Last night I *might* have been practicing my dagger skills with forks—because you can never be too prepared—and broke those glass candleholders on the wall. And then she *might* have caught me trying to climb the staircase, using just the gargoyles and wall instead of the stairs."

"Forks?" Bella says.

"Gargoyles?" I say.

"Hey, I was bored. And FYI, gargoyle climbing is way more fun than sitting around studying baroque history."

"No arguing there," I say.

We continue our exploration while Bella takes decorating notes, discovering a library, the main sitting room, numerous bedrooms, the stairwell to the kitchens in the basement—which the cook shoos us out of—and the ballroom stretching into a long rectangle in back of the castle. But no sign of ghosts. I decide Chet's just full of pranks.

"I wonder if this is where they'll have the ball," Bella says.

"A ball?" Chet's brow furrows. "Like a sports tournament?"

"No. Like a big party with dancing and food," I say, laughing. "It's a fairy-tale ball. You should come."

"You bet! Where there is food, there am I."

"Speaking of food," Bella says, finally closing her design book. "I'm starving. All I've had today is icky airplane food and those itsy scones."

On our way back, I pause to study the portraits hanging along the walls. "These must be all the people who lived here. I wonder if any of them were royalty."

Chet points to one of the paintings. "Bet she was a princess."

The lady is wearing a royal-blue dress with gold beads around the neckline and a crown resting on her head. She appears so lifelike, as if she could stand up and step out of the portrait.

"She seems sad," I say.

"Probably lonely." Bella hooks her arm around mine. "She didn't have such an awesome best friend like you do."

"Come on," Chet says. "How about we sweet-talk that cranky cook into giving us some food?"

I'm turning away when I notice the eyes on the painting shift to stare at me. Her mouth moved and I could have sworn she said, *"Help."*

Panicked, I jerk around to face the portrait again, tightly gripping Bella.

"Guys!" My voice comes out breathless. I back away, pulling Bella along. "Did you see that?"

Chet's eyebrows rise. "You all right? You look like you're going to puke."

"The painting!" My hand shakes as I point. But Chet and Bella only stare at me like I've lost it. I glance from one to the other. "You didn't see anything?"

They shake their heads.

Squinting, I inch closer to the painting. The lady's gaze is back to staring off into nowhere.

"I probably imagined it." I rub my eyes. "Probably jet lag. I read it does weird things to you."

"It's okay." Bella squeezes my arm. "Let's go harass that cook."

But Chet doesn't say a word. I look back at him as he pauses by the painting, tugging on his earlobe before running to catch up with us.

I can't help but wonder if Chet is right. Perhaps this castle really is haunted.

5

Fact: Ghosts are most decidedly not real.

I awake to a world so black I have to blink my eyes repeatedly to see if they're actually open. Where am I?

When I move to sit up, something smacks me on the head. *Ouch!* I jerk around, flailing my arms through the air. A hand slaps against mine. I scream. Someone is next to me! Then that someone starts screaming, too.

Wait. I know that voice. "Bells!" I say, now becoming oriented. The two of us are sharing a bed. In a castle. In France! "Stop screaming. You scared the stars out of me."

I slide off the bed and, after groping through the darkness, find the lamp and yank on its cord. A light glow illuminates the room. Bella sits huddled in the canopy bed, looking a little lost in the pillows and blankets.

"Too bright!" Bella groans, obviously grouchy from being smacked awake. "You're the one who manhandled me and woke me up."

"Sorry." I twist the strings of my pajama pants. "I was having this horrible dream and when I woke up, I couldn't remember where I was. Your hand hit my eye, and I, well, thought you were like a zombie attacking me."

More groaning, and then Bella sits up. "Zombie? Geez, you do have a wild imagination. No wonder you want to be a writer."

A gust of wind courses through the castle, moaning. I freeze, and the memory of the princess staring at me from the portrait flashes before my mind.

"Did you hear that?" I whisper.

She shrugs it off. "Yeah." She leans down and pulls out a pack of crackers and her notepad from her suitcase sitting on the floor. "Sounded like wind. Maybe someone left a window open."

I creep to the door and press my ear to it. "It came from the hall. I think that's the noise that woke me."

"Girl, it's a castle. Everybody knows castles are cold and drafty. Want one?" She holds out a cracker.

I stare hard at my best friend. Bells is right. I'm being silly. I move to grab the cracker, when the grandfather clock downstairs begins to chime with its loud gonging sound. Then a door slams out in the hall, shaking the wooden floor.

"What's up with people slamming their doors in the middle of the night?" I whip open our door and storm into the hall. Darkness shrouds every crevice of the castle hall.

Everywhere except the balcony.

A chill ices over me and I stop in my tracks. I try to swallow and call out. But all I can do is stare at the balcony doors gaping open at the end of the hall.

Silvery, iridescent light shimmers on the balcony, casting patterns of whorls and stars on a stone well. Two pillars rising up on either side of the well support a small tiled roof and a bucket dangling on a rope, swaying in the breeze. It reminds me of the kind of well Snow White might have used. I'm sure it hadn't been there earlier. So how did it suddenly appear there now?

I must be dreaming.

A glance over my shoulder tells me my bedroom door is still ajar. I should tell Bella about this. But I'm so curious, I decide not to bother her. Instead, I inch down the hall, a step and then two, my hand trailing along the papered wall. I squint, trying to decide where the light is coming from. A flashlight? A lantern?

No, it has a gleam to it. And then I realize the light is coming from *inside* the well. My chest constricts and my mouth goes dry. A buzz rings through my eardrums like a warning alarm saying *Go back!*

Still, I press closer.

Stop! I scream to myself. My heart starts thumping because there's something not quite right about this. I try to lock my legs, but they keep moving me closer and closer to the unearthly light. Then, without warning, the light gathers into a spiral and shoots into the hall. It swooshes and gusts around me like a whirlwind.

The gust pulls me to the edge of the well. My hair slaps against my cheeks as I grip its stone edge, rough and solid beneath my palms. The light trickling up from inside the well sparkles like diamond dust. I try to back away, but the light holds me tightly in place.

Round and round the wind circles my body, and then, to my horror, yanks me inside the well. It happens so quickly, I don't have time to scream.

I plummet into the well, shooting as though I'm slipping down a waterslide tunnel. The wind howls, and though I try to hold my hands out to stop myself, it's useless.

With a giant thud, I plop onto my bed! The covers flounce about me as my body drops hard onto the mattress. I wince in pain, but remain absolutely still. Did I just wake up from a dream? What happened? Where is Bella?

Everything in the room feels off-kilter, yet I can't explain why. The room has the same decor, same furniture, same fireplace.

But not.

The door swings open. I expect it to be Bella. But it isn't. It's a girl, panting heavily. She's slightly older than me, with light skin and strands of blond hair braided to form a crown on top of her head and the rest trailing down her back. She wears a huge puffy dress that looks like something from the Middle Ages. Her forehead's bunched up and sweat trickles down the sides of her face.

"Thou hast come! My birthday wish hath cometh true!" She clasps her hands together as if enraptured. Her words are laced with a strong French accent. "But oh, dear. It is not safe now. Thou must flee!"

"Flee?" I raise my eyebrows. "Why?"

The girl slams the door shut behind her and races to the fireplace. She pulls down on the fire poker, and the back of the fireplace disappears.

"Whoa," I say. "How did you do that?"

"Make haste!" The girl waves her hands frantically.

Slowly, I edge off the bed, eyeing the weirdly dressed girl. There's something oddly familiar about her, but I can't figure out what. Still, this girl either knows me somehow or is completely wacked out. If I can manage to slip from the room when she isn't looking, I can find my mom or Madame. The girl obviously needs help.

"I don't understand." My heartbeat kicks up a notch as I creep toward the door. "Who are you?"

"Thou art most certainly not what I was expecting, but that is nary a worry." The girl grabs me by the elbow and literally drags me to the fireplace. "Come hither!"

"Let go of me!" I fight against her.

She twists me around so I'm facing her. When I see the intensity of her expression, I stop resisting.

"Thou must promise to return when it is safer," she says. "I beseech thee not to tarry!"

"Right. How about we go talk to Madame first?"

"The creatures, they smell thy scent. Run, for thy life depends upon it. They have been ordered to kill thee."

"What?" I step away from her. This girl is most definitely a wacko. With a big, fat O. "For a second there, I thought you said *kill*."

Something smashes against the bedroom door. It shudders from the weight of whatever is on the other side. The girl's eyes widen. She snatches the lantern off the mantel and pushes me into the opening inside the fireplace while I'm still eyeing the door.

The girl takes off in a sprint down the narrow passageway. Dust and cobwebs riddle the path. Should I trust her? The bedroom door groans and buckles as something smashes against the door's surface. Then the sound of claws scratching through the wood sends my pulse racing. I swallow back a scream and take off down the secret passageway, batting aside sticky cobwebs and choking on dust.

"What was that back there?" I say as we duck around corners, up three steps, and then down ten more. It's like a rabbit's trail, winding and twisting through the castle until we reach another door with the symbol of two intersecting *W*s carved into its surface.

I halt when I see that symbol. It, too, is oddly familiar. Before I can place it, the girl shoves open the door and we stumble out of a small shed into a garden. A light mist trails over the ground, and moonlight bathes the area.

"Dost thou see that light hanging on the oak?" I nod. "Run to it as fast as thou can."

"But—" My eyes bounce between the girl and the tree. "You need to tell me what's going on. Are my mom and Bella okay?"

The girl's face contorts as if I were asking the strangest questions. "Return when it is safe, for I am desperate for thine assistance! Now make haste!"

The shed door crashes open. A massive shadow leaps out onto the dewy grass. A growl fills the air. I spin on my heels, heart thumping in my chest, and race for the lone lantern swaying in the breeze on one of the oak's boughs.

The lantern's glimmering light closes around me, swirling like an endless eddy. Then in a rush, it yanks me upward just as claws swipe at my bare feet.

My breath squeezes out of me as I shoot into the starry sky. Air swallows my scream, and wind presses against my cheeks.

Then I land. This time with a thump on the hard tiled floor outside of my room, smacking the back of my head. The light churns around me as if licking my skin before sweeping up the chimney and into the hall fireplace. In a final gush, a pull sucks all the air from the room.

Bam! The doors to the balcony crash shut as my lungs gasp for air.

Breathe! I tell myself. *Must breathe.*

But I can't. *No air!* The hall spins.

Then, like springs, every bedroom door along the hall pops open. Air floods back into my lungs. I gulp it in, starved for oxygen.

"What in heavens was that?" Mrs. Jones shrills from her doorway, her curlers trembling.

Mr. Jones stomps out into the hall. "All this noise," he barks. "How is a man supposed to get sleep, eh?"

Meanwhile, Bella and Mom race to me, hunching down on either side of me. Mom's face pales whiter than a moon.

"Keira!" Mom's voice is high-pitched in panic. "What happened? Why are you out here?"

"Oh, wow," Bella says. "Your foot is bleeding."

"I bumped my head," I say, not really knowing the answer to my mom's question. What *did* happen? But after our break-in, Mom has been panicking over the slightest thing and this is supposed to be our vacation away from the chaos back home. "I must have been sleepwalking. Cut myself on something."

"I wondered where you went," Bella says. "Your scream scared me."

"Are you okay?" Mom's hands shake as she cradles my face with them. "Tell me you're okay!"

The scratch on my foot keeps bleeding, dripping onto the floor. I dare a glance at the fireplace at the end of the hall, but it appears harmless. "Yeah. I guess."

But I'm not. And from Mom's expression, my lying skills haven't improved either. I want to tell her what happened, but how do I explain what I saw? The *WW* symbol pushes into my mind, nagging at me.

"Don't you worry," Mom says. "We'll get some antiseptic for that and a Band-Aid."

With the help of Bella and Mom, I stand and hobble toward our room. Moonlight streams in through the windowpanes of the balcony's closed doors. It's as if nothing happened.

"All that banging noise, it was you, wasn't it?" Mr. Jones points a gnarly finger at me. The guy just won't give it up. "Waking us up from a peaceful sleep."

"You don't talk to my daughter that way!" Mom says sharply.

"She doesn't look so good." Mr. Parker comes over to us and adjusts his spectacles as if to get a better look at me. "Looks like she's seen a ghost."

"I thought I saw something on the balcony." My voice trembles.

"I'll check it out." Chet hurries over and swings open the balcony doors with a flourish.

Nothing is there.

"Must have imagined it," I mumble.

Madame scurries into the center of the hall, one hand clasping a candle in front of her chest. "Please calm down!" She waves her free hand in the air. "Do not worry yourselves. We have such drafts here. Especially in the early summer."

"But it isn't even windy outside," Mrs. Jones says.

"Yes, well, it comes in bursts." Madame bustles to the end of the hall, pushes Chet aside, and closes the doors. Then she slips one of her silver keys into the keyhole of the balcony doors and twists it. "There. All locked up. Nothing to worry yourself over."

"That's not what I've heard," growls Mr. Jones. "The townsfolk say the castle is haunted. Plus, what about last night? There were noises then, too."

Madame glares at him, her face shadowed in the candle-light. "You shouldn't listen to such rumors," she warns before marching back to her room.

"So there *are* rumors!" Mrs. Jones calls after Madame's retreating form. Madame's answer is the slam of a door.

"Do you want to sleep in my room tonight?" Mom asks.

"No, I'm fine," I say, attempting to be brave. I hook arms with Bella. "Bells will keep me company."

But as I step into our bedroom, I make sure to lock the door. Because now I know the rumors are true.

Survival Fact: To leave a dragon's lair unscathed, remember to wear fire-resistant clothing.

SATURDAY (SAMEDI), JUNE 12TH

Breakfast is a solemn affair. No one utters a word, most certainly not a whisper about last night. All I hear is the clinking of silverware, Bella's pencil scratching on her design book, Chet slurping his water, and the rustling of Mr. Parker's newspaper as he turns the pages, clearly ignoring Chet.

"Excellent news," Mom says from across the table. "According to the local paper, there was an unexpected storm last night that blew down some telephone poles. Isn't it reassuring to have science and facts to explain things like what happened last night?"

"Wasn't that in the South of France?" Mr. Jones says gruffly.

"Yes." Mom shifts uneasily in her chair. "But there may have been aftereffects that reached here."

"Do you actually think the storm in Southern France made the doors in our rooms shut like that?" Mrs. Jones says doubtfully. "That sounds quite odd."

The last thing I want to talk about is last night. When I lay down, I couldn't stop thinking about it, hardly sleeping a wink, so now I can barely keep my eyes open as I take a bite of croissant.

That is, until the door to the dining room smashes open, revealing a slender woman with a fitted pinstripe suit and spike heels. But it's the woman's hair that catches my attention. A flaming red that flings out like dragon's breath as she sails into the room. I literally jump in my chair, while Mrs. Jones drops her tea in shock. The china crashes onto the wooden floor and splinters into shards.

"Good heavens!" Mrs. Jones cries out. "What is the meaning of this? You scared my hair straight!"

The woman responsible merely bats her eyes, holding both palms before her.

"Apologies for startling you," she says, and then clasps her hands together. "But I'm just so eager to meet our *dearest* Keira and her *lovely* friend Isabella. The princesses of the week. I'm Ms. Teppernat from *Girls' World*. We talked on the phone."

Bella and I glance at each other. Bella lifts an eyebrow skeptically while I bite back a giggle. No one has ever called me "dearest," and perhaps Bella could pass for a princess, but I most definitely am too much of a tomboy to fit into that category. But somehow I manage a polite smile once again.

"And what a lovely drawing!" Ms. Teppernat exclaims as she leans over Bella's shoulder to study the drawing. "It appears that we have a writer and an illustrator amongst us."

"Actually, I'm an interior designer," Bella says, glowing from the compliment. "Currently, I'm redesigning the entire castle in my design book with a modern decor."

"Fascinating! Pleasure to meet you." Ms. Teppernat holds out her hand and Bella shakes it.

"Aren't we so civilized," Bella whispers to me. "Shaking hands and drinking from china teacups at eight in the morning."

Before I can answer, Madame raps her cane twice on the floor.

"Enough!" Madame says darkly from her end of the table.

She sits up straight, her arms positioned on the armrests like she's a queen on a throne. I must say I'm impressed. In less than five seconds, the housekeeper has the entire table under her control. "Next time you come for a visit, do remember to knock."

"Naturally, of course," Ms. Teppernat says, but her smile wanes and her eyes narrow at Madame. Then she clears her throat and snaps her fingers to a lady beside her who I guess to be Ms. Teppernat's assistant.

Promptly, the assistant hands over a folder and clipboard. Her long black hair is tucked up into a bun and three pencils are jammed into it. She wears a tight blue shirt and pencil skirt with brown walking shoes. A pink apron full of pockets protects her outfit. The pockets brim with spools of thread, mini scissors, and sewing needles. A notepad swings from a string attached to her apron.

"Miss Keira and Miss Isabella," Ms. Teppernat says. "We have a rigorous schedule set out for you and less than one week to accomplish our prestigious agenda. I hope you're prepared for a week of royal elegance and entertainment. Cheryl, go ahead and pass out the lists to our princesses."

I swallow as Cheryl, the assistant, places a list before Bella and me.

"I'd like to have a copy of that list as well," Mom says eagerly.

I glance over the schedule:

Schedule for Fairy-Tale Storytelling Contest

> *Saturday: Reenact arrival at the castle. Lost slipper on castle steps. (Cinderella theme)*

> * *Order ice sculpture for ball. Something fairy tale-ish. Pumpkin, slipper, spinning wheel, apple . . .*

Sunday: Horseback riding! (The Goose Girl theme)

> * *Confirm guest list*

Monday: ~~Boating~~ (Weather report calls for rain) French cooking class (Snow White theme)

> * *Ball gown fitting*

Tuesday: Boating and picnic (Little Mermaid theme)

Wednesday: French etiquette and cultural study (Beauty and the Beast theme)

Thursday: Dance lessons (Twelve Dancing Sisters theme)

> * *Note: still need to find a suitable instructor*

Friday: The grand ball!

I stare at the list, my stomach twisting at the rigorous schedule. "But when do I get to see the sights here?" I say.

"I love this!" Mom says. "I've always said no good trip comes without a well-laid-out plan of action. I'm thrilled to see how organized and thorough you are."

"That's what we do best!" Ms. Teppernat beams as if she had just kissed Prince Charming. "And for the rest of you. Please do know you are all welcome to join us for the grand fairy-tale ball this Friday. It's destined to be absolutely magical!"

"I've always wanted to attend a ball," Bella says, her face shining. "It sounds divine."

"Perhaps we shall have our very own designer restyle the ballroom for the event." Ms. Teppernat focuses on Bella. "How does that sound to you?"

"An excellent idea." The assistant nods vigorously, relief flooding her features. She pulls out her notepad and a pencil from her bun and starts scribbling down notes. "We could feature her designs in the magazine."

"Wow," Bella says. "That would be grand. I can already envision the palette of colors I'll use."

"Perfect!" Ms. Teppernat sighs in delight. "It's all settled, then."

"Hold on. A ball?" Madame rises from her throne. "I never authorized a ball."

"Of course you didn't," Ms. Teppernat says. "I did. Monsieur Monteque approved it. He said it would be good for others to see what a lovely château you all have here."

"That's preposterous!" Madame says. Honestly, I'm surprised flames didn't burst out of Ms. Teppernat's mouth at Madame's response. Who needs TV when you can watch real live dragons in action? "He would never authorize such an event. I must speak to him at once before you go gallivanting about."

"Fine!" Ms. Teppernat practically snarls. "Talk to him. And then you'll see I was right. Come along, Keira. It's time for your makeup and costume."

"Makeup and costume?" I stand ever so slowly. Bella cringes and clasps my hand, knowing how I'm not into that kind of stuff.

"You can do this." She squeezes my hand as Cheryl whips out a measuring tape and begins to measure all my body parts.

"Man," Chet tells me, whistling, "that's rough. But after you're done, come find me. I think I discovered something you'll find interesting."

*Fact about Dragons: Dragons aren't real,
so we won't waste our time discussing them.*

So I'm sweating on the castle's front steps in a dress that looks like something from *Romeo and Juliet*. (Don't ask.) Waiting.

It's all Ms. Teppernat's fault. She's the lead from *Girls' World* on this article. When she marched into the castle this morning unannounced and appearing like Maleficent, I actually considered canceling this whole thing. The massive itinerary has me freaking out. And I'm to be filmed and photographed at the grand ball! There's a whole crew of people to photograph me, and all the fuss makes me want to dive off the drawbridge. The only time I'm ever been photographed is either for school pictures or when my dad takes pictures during my soccer tournaments.

As Cheryl instructs me on basic poses, all I can think about is what happened last night and the strange similarities to the girl I met and the one in my story. Maybe I had been sleep-walking. Or dreaming. But honestly, I think I really did enter a secret passageway in the castle. And even though I can't remember exactly how that strange girl opened the fireplace, I'm determined to find out.

"Hurry, everyone!" Ms. Teppernat yells to the crew. "Let's get this shot wrapped up."

But everything comes to a halt when Madame struts out to meet Ms. Teppernat on the bridge, fists clenched as if she were marching into battle.

"You are disregarding my rules!" Madame says.

"I *told* you on the phone, the shoot won't last more than an hour." Ms. Teppernat looms over Madame in her spike heels.

"I am hardly worried about your measly photography shoots." Madame lifts her chin as if she's the queen of France. "It is Friday that is bothersome."

"Bothersome?" Ms. Teppernat yanks her sunglasses off and glares down at Madame as if her eyes have a special power. "You should have checked the calendar before booking us. I've already arranged a whole crew. Events must proceed as planned."

"I will call Monsieur, then." Madame's tone carries with it a threat as she reenters the castle.

"Then call him!" Ms. Teppernat snarls as the giant door slams shut.

Pivoting on the points of her heels, Ms. Teppernat clicks her way across the bridge toward me and the camera crew. Her sunglasses sway at her side as her lips stretch into a victorious smile.

"Wonderful!" Ms. Teppernat claps her hands lightly. "Everyone is ready and waiting. But, Keira, *please*, the slouching is so unprincess-like."

Cheryl hands Ms. Teppernat her clipboard, which Ms. Teppernat in turn reads and begins shouting out orders. This was the deal. I get to come on a magical holiday with my best friend and Mom as long as I model for the fairy-tale spread that *Girls' World* will print along with my story. I really have nothing to complain about.

So I pose with a suitcase in front of the castle, reenacting my arrival. Next, I run up the stairs, pretending to lose my shoe. Who knew it would be so hard to purposely lose a shoe?

"It just won't come off by itself," I try to explain.

"Mercies!" Ms. Teppernat says. "Shoe loss shouldn't be this difficult. Keira, you must channel Cinderella. Feel how she must have felt. Cheryl! Get this girl some heels or something that will fall off easily."

While Cheryl races off to the *Girls' World* trailer, I attempt to channel Cinderella, but all I can think about is last night. I need answers.

Solid, hard facts. Which is very bad because now I'm sounding just like my mom!

"Not a frown, dear," Ms. Teppernat calls out. "A look of awe. There, that's better."

Click, click. The photographers move around me.

"Lovely! Now let's get a picture of you standing without the luggage in the front of the castle. Nice."

I turn and spy Chet flying down the path on some kind of contraption that resembles a skateboard. Knowing him, he made it himself from scavenged parts. His arms are stretched out for balance and his tongue touches his upper lip as if he's in deep concentration. He must have hit a rock or an upturned cobblestone, because just as he rounds the garden path, the board jerks upward, sending him sailing into the perfectly squared hedge of bushes edging the entrance to the bridge.

He lands with a grunt and then there's a loud screech. A person pops out of the bushes beside him with flailing arms. The hat covering curly white hair and the sunglasses may have hidden the eyes, but there's no mistaking who it is.

Old Mother Hubbard.

But why is she hiding in the bushes? My sleuthing instincts kick in. Could she have been spying?

"Insolent boy!" Mrs. Jones brushes leaves from her paisley-patterned dress, all the while muttering under her breath.

"What in heaven's name is going on?" Ms. Teppernat asks, frowning at Chet's two sneakers sticking into the air.

Chet rights himself, springs to his feet, and flourishes a grand bow to his newfound audience. A grin stretches across his face. The camera crew bursts into applause.

"He's a daredevil, that boy." Ms. Teppernat taps her manicured finger against her lips. "Might be useful."

No one spares an awfully spry Old Mother Hubbard a second glance as she scrambles out of the bushes, hops over the hedge, and darts across the lawn toward the east garden, binoculars dangling around her neck.

No one, that is, except me.

8

*Fairy-Tale Tidbit: In the Grimm brothers' Frog Prince,
he turns into a prince not through the princess's kiss but
when she throws him against a wall in utter disgust.*

"Keira! Keira!"

Bella is running wildly across the pristine lawn, her dangle earrings bobbing against her shoulders.

"Hey," I say. "Is something wrong?"

"Yes!" Bella bends over, panting. "I mean no. Well, sort of. I've been looking for you everywhere."

"I just finished that photo shoot. What's going on?"

"Everyone's talking about it back at the castle." She scrunches up her nose. "Did you hear yet?"

"No! Spill it already."

"One of the maids went missing last night. Everyone's looking for her."

"You don't really believe she went missing." I brush the grass from my medieval-style dress. "Maybe she decided to quit. I wouldn't blame her. I think I'd die if I had to work under Madame."

"She is scary, isn't she? I'm starting to think she really *is* the Wicked Witch of the West." Bella sighs and hooks arms with me. "Maybe you're right. Still, isn't the thought of the castle being haunted deliciously creepy?"

"Um. Actually, no." A shiver slides down my spine as I remember the terror of racing through the secret passageways last night.

We head to the low wall that looks over the Cher River and perch ourselves on it. Just before us, the castle's white walls scrape against the blue sky. Gables and fluted turrets emit a romantic air, and I can totally imagine a princess standing on the balcony, waving to her prince.

"Speaking of strange things, something odd happened during the photo shoot," I say, and then I tell her about Mrs. Jones's strange behavior.

"Sounds like she was bird-watching or studying plant life."

"Maybe." I jump down from the railing. "But I'm going to find out."

"Find out what exactly? You're scaring me."

"Don't be silly. I'm just going to do a little investigating."

Darting ahead, Bella blocks the door of the castle. "Oh no, you're not. Your curiosity always gets you—or should I say both of us—in trouble."

Bella may have a point. When a dress collection of Ms. Francois's went missing, my first guess was that the neighbors were the culprit. I decided to conduct my own investigation. Bella helped me tie a rope from her second-story room. I planned to use it to swing across to the neighbor's house and grab their drain pipe. Unfortunately, my grip slipped and I swung backward and barreled through the Francois's kitchen window. It took nearly a year of my allowance to pay for damages.

I sidestep Bella and pull on the thick door handle, only to find it quickly opened by the butler, who bows low as we enter.

"*Merci*," we say in unison.

But the butler merely moves away to the sitting room in silence. Bella frowns at his retreating form.

"That guy is creepy," she whispers in my ear.

"I don't think he talks. Come on."

All the rooms downstairs are empty except the dining room, where we spy Mr. and Mrs. Jones talking to Madame.

"This is such a worry!" Mrs. Jones is saying, waving her knitting kneedles through the air. "The cook said she was here one moment, and the next—whoosh! She simply vanished!"

"Highly irregular." Mr. Jones nods in that rooster-pecking way of his. "We are deeply concerned for our safety and that of the other guests. Have you ever considered closing this château to visitors?"

"Of course not! I am sure that is not what happened," Madame says drily. "Cook has a tendency for dramatics."

"They're distracted," I whisper. "Perfect."

I rush back down the main hall and then up the staircase with Bella at my heels.

"What are we doing?" She squeaks out her words. "And do you think we should worry about one of the maids going missing?"

"I'm sure it's nothing. The maid probably got sick of hearing Mrs. Jones complain all the time. Besides, Mrs. Jones is up to something and I'm going to find out what."

"Don't even go there. Remember the time when you thought Mrs. Nickels killed her cat? Or when we were sent to the principal's office for sneaking into the cafeteria?"

"They were serving outdated food!" I peek into the upstairs hall. It's empty. "We'd never have gotten caught if I hadn't accidently spilled the chocolate pudding."

Bella snickers. "That was kinda funny. You sprawled on the ground, covered in chocolate. Even your face—"

I glare at her. She bites on her lips to stop giggling, but it really doesn't work all that well.

Since the hall is clear, I tiptoe to outside the Joneses' room and turn the doorknob.

Locked. No biggie. Locks never stopped me before.

I hurry to our room and dig through the desk. Thankfully, I find a paper clip stuck at the back of the top drawer. Back at the Joneses, it doesn't take long before I wiggle the paper clip into the lock, and Bella and I slip inside their room. There are two suitcases tucked in the corner. The bed is crisply made, not a hint of wrinkles. The dresser holds a lamp, hairbrush, and two books. I pick one up. *Manuel de l'immobilier.* Boring! I put it back in place and look at the other. *The World's Scariest Ghost Stories.* Cool.

They're both library books. Overdue ones at that.

I check the library location. Paris, France? But I thought the Joneses were from England. It could mean something. Or it could mean that this book was left here by a random French guest.

Other than that, the room appears annoyingly barren. I slide open one of the dresser drawers to find a pile of shirts, folded in neat rectangles. I check out another drawer. Socks. I wrinkle my nose. Not so clean socks actually.

"I still don't get why we're going through the Joneses' stuff." Bella rubs her hands together nervously. "I don't know about France, but it's against the law in the States without a warrant."

"Evidence." I drop to my knees and slip under the bed. Dust balls and sneakers. "Hard-core evidence."

The door creaks, startling me. I bang my head on the underside of the bed.

"Ouch!" I mutter.

"Don't tell me," a boy's voice says. It sounds painfully like Chet's. "You're hunting for rats. If so, you're in the wrong room. There is one room downstairs that's got a whole nest of them."

"A nest?" Bella's voice quivers. "Of rats?"

I peek my head out from under the bed. Yep. It is Chet, leaning against the doorframe, looking smug.

I blow a dust ball off my nose and wipe loose strands of hair away from my eyes as I stand, chin raised. "We aren't looking for rats. Besides, if we were, it wouldn't be any of your business. Now if you'll be so kind and find your manners and leave us be."

"My manners?" He crosses his arms. "Here you're rummaging through another person's stuff and I'm the one who needs manners. This is really confusing."

I grab Bella by the wrist and attempt to squeeze past Chet, but he moves sideways and blocks the whole door.

"You're in our way," I point out.

There's that mischievous smile again. "Why, yes, I am."

Voices coming from the staircase echo down the hallway. They sound just like the Joneses! My eyes widen. Bella squeezes my hand.

"Please, Chet," Bella says. "Just let us out."

"No sweat. Tell me why you're snooping around in their room and I'll let you little criminals out."

"That's bribery," I huff. "That's illegal."

"You're trespassing," he says. "That's illegal, too."

"Fine." I glower at Chet. "Just let us out!"

Chet moves back and flourishes his hand for us to pass like he's some kind of knight trying to be chivalrous. Bella shuts the door just as Mrs. Jones crests the top of the stairs, with Mr. Jones coming behind limping slightly and wheezing.

"Sweet honey and jam!" Her eyes narrow. "Whatever are you doing outside my room?"

"Mrs. Jones!" I step toward her. "We were looking for you. I must have knocked on your door a thousand times. We had nearly given up."

"Dear me, this seems rather serious. Whatever could be the problem?"

I bite my lip. I'd sunk so deep, I didn't know how to get out.

"Binoculars," I find myself saying. "We spotted this lovely bird in one of the trees and wondered if you had a pair for us to use."

"I am terribly sorry," Mrs. Jones says in a voice that sounds as if she's most decidedly not sorry. "I don't have a set. Try one of the shops in town."

The Joneses hurry into their room, slamming the door with a loud thud.

I shoot a pointed look at Bella. "See! She's lying. She totally had binoculars this morning," I say. "Something's up."

"Can't wait to hear all about it," Chet says meaningfully.

"You are evil." I scowl at him. "Pure evil."

"Hey," Chet says. "I'll take that over boring any day."

The door pops back open. Mrs. Jones holds Bella's design journal in the air. "Excuse me, girls, did one of you drop this in my room?"

9

Fact: The first recorded librarian was a Greek scholar named Zenodotus who lived 1,100 years before the first book was even printed. Talk about before his time!

I plop into the library armchair after the Jones fiasco. The library has that melancholy, serious feel, with mahogany furniture, wood-paneled walls, and a ceiling painted plum. Normally, it would've soothed me, except I still have Mrs. Jones's glare imprinted on my memory.

"Okay, people," I tell Chet and Bella. "What are we going to do about Mrs. Jones?"

"What do you mean 'we'?" Chet asks, inspecting the coat of arms hanging on the wall. "You two were the ones snooping around in there, not me."

Bella shakes her head. "We are so dead."

"Naw." Chet pulls the knight's helmet off a suit of armor. "She's just an old lady. What can she do to you?"

"That's my whole point!" I shoot up from the chair. "Madame and my mom will totally believe her when she tells them we were in her room."

"You're acting like you were in the right." Chet's voice is muffled from behind the helmet visor.

"By the way," I say. "This morning at breakfast, you said you had something to show us."

"Don't think I want to show you anymore."

"That's juvenile," I say.

"Fine. But it means from now on, you have to let me in on all of your sleuthing expeditions."

"We don't do *expeditions*." Bella rolls her eyes as she digs through her bag. "It's not like hiking a mountain."

"It's a deal!" I say before Chet changes his mind and hold out my hand.

"Okay. Cool." Chet gives me a solid handshake and then withdraws a thin silver key from his pocket. "I found this on the floor outside of Madame's room."

"What do you think it opens?" Bella sets her bag aside to inspect the key.

"Don't know, but you bet I'm going to find out!" Chet spins the key through his fingers. "Maybe it opens the door where she keeps the ghosts inside?"

"You think Madame has something to do with the ghosts?" Bella asks.

"Maybe." Chet tugs on his earlobe, considering.

"I'll make a list," I offer. I go to the desk and pull out a pen and paper, but pause.

The memory of when I last used a pen to create a plan storms back at me. Grandma's special pen. The one hidden safely upstairs in my room.

"Maybe you should make up a list of ideas." I hold out the paper and pen to Bella, needing time to think. She gives me an odd look, but takes them.

There's no doubt Grandma's pen is special, but could it truly be magical? Could it help me solve this ghost problem? I consider this as I wander to the bookshelves that stretch from floor to ceiling, soaking in that smell of old books. Everything about this room reminds me of my visits to Grandma's house, when we used to secretly read together. Mom never approved of fiction stories, so it had always been so much fun hanging out with Grandma.

A track runs along the ceiling where a moving ladder hooks into it, just like in the movie *Beauty and the Beast*. I grip the sides and step up on the first rung. A tingle spreads through my fingers and up my arms.

"That was weird." I wiggle my fingers.

"It's time you fess up," Chet says, ignoring me. "I told you about the key. Why were you going through the Joneses' stuff?"

"You know, Keira"—Bella looks up triumphantly from her bag—"I wasn't buying that Jones hunch of yours. But now that I think about it, maybe you're onto something."

"You think so?"

"And sure, you were dead wrong about the cat killer, but you were totally right about the chocolate pudding."

"Cat killer?" Chet says. "Chocolate pudding? What are you two talking about?"

I shake my head. "Long story."

"You may not have found evidence, but *voilà*!" Bella pulls out a hairnet from her bag and dangles it above her head. "I did!"

"A hairnet!" I say as if Bella had whipped out the Golden Fleece.

"A hairnet?" Chet laughs. "You two are killing me."

"You're brilliant, Bells!" I say.

"Why, thank you." She blows me a kiss.

"I'm completely lost," Chet says.

"If she found a hairnet, there's a strong possibility Mrs. Jones uses it to hold her hair under a wig," I say, stepping higher on the ladder. "There was a heap of makeup in one of the drawers, now that I think of it. Do you think Mrs. Jones is dressed in disguise?"

Bella shrugs. "It's a possibility."

"Old ladies lose hair," Chet argues. "They wear wigs."

"Are you sure she's old?" I try to push the ladder along the bookshelves. But it's jammed. "I mean, how many elderly people do you see leaping into bushes? Hey, Chet, can you give me a little push? I think the ladder is stuck."

The grandfather clock down the hall starts chiming, the noise vibrating so loud it shakes the walls.

"That clock is messed up," Bella says. "It rings at the strangest times!"

Chet tries to turn around with the helmet still on his head but, unable to see where he's going, ends up stumbling and falls into the ladder. With a jerk, the ladder breaks free from the groove it had been jammed in and starts sliding along the bookshelves. I grip tight, expecting it to slow down. Except it doesn't. It speeds up.

And that's when a surprising thing happens.

The wall at the end of the bookshelf opens, allowing a stream of white light to burst out as if reaching for me.

I clutch the ladder rungs, my knuckles bone-white. I should jump off, scream, anything but allow myself to go fly-ing into that open space. But it's as if my fingers are glued to the ladder.

To my left, Chet's visor is pushed up and he's staring wide-eyed at me, while Bella shouts out my name. Both of them leap, trying to stop the ladder from continuing down its tracks into the unknown. They're too slow.

I fly straight into the shock of light, and they vanish from sight.

Fact: ~~Fairies are known to cause mischief.~~
Note: Fairies are completely fictional,
so please disregard this fact.

I'm flung from the ladder and tumble across the muddy ground. Thankfully, mud is soft and forgiving. I sit up and wipe away the sludge from my face. It takes a few moments to get my bearings. The castle walls rise up just across the river. In fact, it appears as if I landed in the garden right across the moat.

Weird.

I blink a few times, trying to understand what happened. The only explanation for this is I hit my head against the wall after Chet pushed the ladder. I must have been knocked out and now I'm dreaming.

A wave of dizziness tumbles through my body as I attempt standing. I stumble to the bushes to throw up. My dress is torn and streaked with mud. It's a good thing I'm dreaming; otherwise, Cheryl would have a heart attack.

I'm about to slump back to the ground when a girl rushes over to me, panic filling her big eyes. Wait a second. She's the same girl from my dream last night! Today she's wearing a long pink dress, puffed out like a bell. White ribbons are woven around the skirt and up her bodice. Her hair is curled into ringlets and pinned back with flower barrettes.

"Thou hast returned!" The girl runs up and hugs me. I pat her awkwardly on the back. "I've been wishing upon a star every night since thou escaped."

"Um—thanks? Where am I? And who are you?"

"But I am Gabrielle, dost thou not remember?" The girl clucks her tongue while shaking her head. "Now let us not be foolish. I know thee and thou knowest me. Clearly. So heed the plan. We shall proceed directly to the party and thou shall attempt to work out who it is that schemes to capture us and take us to the Dark Tower. Then we shall meet afterward to find a way to stop them."

My body freezes momentarily, and my mind whirls. I don't even protest when Gabrielle begins to drag me down the oak path.

Dark Tower. She keeps talking about that. I glance around, wondering if there are any more of those creatures nearby that nearly tore the door apart and chased me.

Second, her name nags me. *Gabrielle.* Is it just a coincidence that it is the exact same name as the princess in the fairy tale I wrote for the contest? And that the princess in my story was captured in the same way? And how did the girl even know me?

"Princess Gabrielle?" I say breathlessly, hoping she will tell me I'm wrong.

The girl giggles. "Of course! Thou art most assuredly not what I was expecting. But I like thee."

Yep. I'm definitely dreaming. After all, what are the odds that I'd pick the exact name as her? It won't be long before I wake up with a huge bump on my forehead and a terrible headache. Meanwhile, the girl continues to talk about the guests and who she thinks are the prime suspects.

We turn off the main path and enter a wide grove filled with at least fifty people dressed in similar fashion to the girl, drinking from teacups and eating delicacies. Tables edge the forest like flowered hedges, filled with towering cakes and plates of delicate macaroons. Fresh-flower streamers stretch between the oaks. Bands of blue and yellow material are woven together and sway from the tree boughs.

My heart dips. This is exactly how I imagined the party my character attends in my fairy tale. I suck in a deep breath, pressing my fingers to my forehead. I just need a moment to wrap my mind around why I'm dreaming about this part.

Except that's kind of hard when Princess Gabrielle is handing me a large ball.

"Keep a good eye out for anyone who looks suspicious," the princess whispers.

I stare at the ball, completely baffled. Does Gabrielle want me to hit the killer with this?

"Whatever is the matter? It is thy turn to play." Princess Gabrielle's ringlets bounce as she laughs. "Thou dost know the rules of *pétanque*? Throw the ball and attempt to get as close as possible to the smaller ball over there."

"Riiiight," I say, eyeing the group of girls giggling over my dress. Not that I blame them. Compared to their big frolicking, frilled skirts, my Renaissance dress—now ripped and muddy—could serve for their servants' dishrags.

I take a deep breath. It's only a matter of time before I wake. I'll go along with things until I do. Besides, why not play some baseball and have a little fun to boot? So I spread my feet apart, turn, and hold the ball against my shoulder like I'm about to throw a baseball.

Gabrielle frowns. "Whatever art thou doing?" she says. "Do not hold it *that* way."

I'm about to ask for more details when I spy Madame strolling through the crowd with two men carrying a large box wrapped with a ribbon and piled high with flowers. Oddly, she isn't wearing her housekeeper outfit but a midnight-blue dress that sways with each step she takes.

"Madame!" I drop the ball, or whatever it is, and race to Madame. "I'm so glad you're here. I'm—"

But I don't utter another word because when Madame turns to face me, it isn't the same woman, or not exactly. Sure, it's still Madame, but she's so much younger! The harsh lines ringing her eyes are washed away and the gray of her hair has vanished.

"Don't think you can get away with this." Madame sneers at me. "I know what you're planning."

I back up. "I don't know what you are talking about."

"And you believe this stunt with your ridiculous dress and games will work?" Madame says, and then cackles. "I think not. You will still lose once again. And your princess is next."

"My princess? I don't understand."

Madame points with her eyes to Gabrielle strolling toward me, her forehead bunched in confusion.

"You're talking about Gabrielle?" I decide this dream is getting weirder by the second.

But Madame merely sniffs. "Tick-tock, little meddler. Listen for the stroke of midnight and perhaps next time you will take me seriously."

"Art thou feeling ill?" Gabrielle touches me lightly on the shoulder. "Thou seemest rather peeked. Here, take some of my smelling salts."

"I'm sorry, I don't think I can help you after all," I say. "And I'll pass on the salts."

"Happy birthday, Gabrielle," Madame says in a sickly sweet voice as she elbows me aside. "I brought you a present."

Madame flourishes her hand, and the two men with white wigs, and the oddest tight pants ever, step forward and present Gabrielle with a box piled high with white flowers. Madame opens the lid to reveal a piano-looking instrument.

"A clavichord!" Gabrielle clasps her hands to her pink cheeks, gasping. "It is simply lovely."

"Yes!" Madame says. "For you to play at the ball."

A clavichord? A ball? I back away from Gabrielle and Madame. This dream keeps getting weirder and weirder. The costumes, my supposed princess, and Madame's crazy threat.

I push my way through the crowd, causing people to gasp in shock at my horrid behavior. But I don't care. My heart starts thumping as if a hammer is banging against it. Something is wrong and I need to wake up. Maybe if I go back to the castle, that would help.

As I break free of the last of the partygoers, I take off into a sprint, not caring that my bare feet are getting sliced up by pebbles and sticks. I skid back out onto the path and pump my arms. But as I round a corner, a cloud of large colorful dragonflies heads in my direction.

And then they are everywhere, swarming down from the whispering trees in a cacophony of colors. Shimmering like a rainbow of falling stars, they dive down directly into my path and start stinging me. I swat them away, but falter when I hear one of them make a *humph* sound.

"The ugly thing thinks she's so big and bad!" one of the dragonflies says.

Squinting, I realize that the dragonfly is actually a miniature person. It's a girl with long wavy purple hair. She floats in the air using iridescent wings. Her ears are pointed and her sharp nose twitches like she smells something disgusting. Her eyes twinkle in a taunting manner as she twirls a spear in her hand as if it's a baton and she's in a parade. She wears a tight purple bodice with tiny gems sewn so closely together that, as they flash, it gives the illusion that the girl's bodice is moving.

I rub my eyes. No, it can't be.

"Fairies?" I say. "But fairies aren't real."

"Does this feel real, slobbery human?" Something jabs me in the neck and then my arm. "Or this? Or this, this, this!"

"Ouch!" I'm flailing my arms around me, but their little spears really hurt. Like bee stings. I bet these fairies put poison in their little spears.

Fairy wingbeats fill the canopied path with a twittering sound that starts to pulse against my ears.

"Go away, go away, and don't come back any other day!" sing the fairies as they titter and poke and swarm until I'm dazed and confused.

I try to remember which way the castle is, but the dizzying fairy wall of colors blocks my sight. They continue to sing the "go away" song as they stab me, each jab reminding me of when I took a sewing class in fifth grade and kept stabbing myself with the needle. Only, this is the nightmare version.

I have no clue which way to run I'm so disoriented, but if I don't go somewhere soon, I'll pass out from their poison. So I take a deep breath and charge through the shimmering wall, running faster than I ever have at a soccer game.

Finally, I stumble back onto the smooth lawn that surrounds the castle, and there right before me stands a large ladder smack in the middle of the green. It sparkles in the sunlight as if someone spilled a bucket of silver glitter over it.

From the polished wood, I can tell that this is the exact ladder I was on in the library before I woke up on the muddy ground. Tentatively, I reach out and touch a rung. A shiver of electricity flows through me just as it had when I first stepped up on it at the library.

I hesitate, unsure if this is the best idea. But then the sound of the swarming fairies permeates the air. They're flooding out of the forest path, so many more than before. I bet they went and got all of their cousins, aunts, uncles, and extra spears. And now they're charging at me for no reason.

Maybe this is how Alice felt entering Wonderland.

I leap onto the ladder, hoping it might be my ticket to waking up. The ladder whips me sideways. Startled, I scream. My hair streams behind me, long and wild, and the wind soaks up my cries. The ladder hurtles toward the castle walls at an alarming speed. I try to jump off, but I can't. My hands are glued to the rungs. I'm going to smash into the white wall! Suddenly, a tunnel of starry light appears, allowing my ladder to slide through.

The light swallows my ladder and me in one gulp.

Fairy-Tale Tidbit: In the brothers' Grimm version of
Cinderella, *a small hazel tree that Cinderella waters
with her tears is what gives her the ball gown.*

I sail off the ladder, roll across a wooden floor, and smash
against the side of a couch.

"Holy fire!" Chet says, lifting the helmet off his head.
"That was wild."

"Keira! Are you okay?" Bella rushes to me and starts
checking my head and arms.

Groaning because every inch of my body hurts from tumbling twice and being stabbed by hundreds of fairies, I drag
my head off the floor and take in my surroundings. I'm back
in the library. Safe. Bella and Chet are here, too. Their eyes
are practically popping out of their sockets.

"I had this crazy dream," I say weakly.

"Dude," Chet says. "I'm sorry for falling on the ladder. I
didn't know it would fly away—"

Then his voice drops off as his gaze wanders to the
back wall.

"What happened?" Bella says. "You went flying on that
ladder when a big light appeared and you got swallowed up
inside. Then a few seconds later, you flew back into the room.
Oh my gosh. That was so scary."

"Wait a sec," I say. "You saw that light? But I thought it was just a dream."

"Oh, we saw it all right," Chet says. Then he stands and picks up the broom lying beside the fireplace and starts poking the back wall where I came through.

"I don't understand." I'm finding it hard to breathe.

"I don't either." Bella wraps me in a hug. "But you're here now. Everything is okay."

"Okay?" Chet says. "I don't think that would be the word I'd use. *Cool*, maybe. *Crazy*, probably. But definitely not *okay*."

The library door swings open and Mom emerges with a scowl on her face.

"There you are!" she says, one hand on her hip, the other on the doorknob. "I thought I heard something in here. I've been looking everywhere for you, Keira. And the library is the last place I expected you to be. How could you break my rule of entering the library without my supervision?"

"I—um—" What do I say? Is it weird that I really, really wish I'd followed Mom's rules after all the stuff I've been experiencing?

Mom's eyes wander to the bookshelves. She inches to the closest shelf and with shaking fingers touches one of the books' spines with incredible reverence. Then her hand snaps away as if the book bit her.

"So many books," Mom says, her voice suddenly quivering. "And pens. And paper."

"I think there are some nonfiction books here," Bella says, moving to Mom's side.

But Bella's words must have jerked Mom from her reverie because she whips around sharply and clears her throat.

"No, I need to leave." Mom backs away toward the door a little unsteadily. "Madame has called us for dinner. Let's not be late. She's in a bad enough mood as it is."

Madame. Just the mention of her sends a tremor through me. She is the only common thread between my bizarre experience and reality.

"Good," I say. "Because I need to talk to Madame as soon as possible."

* * *

Dinner is a formal affair with a linen tablecloth, tall candles poised in silver candelabras, and so many forks and spoons it's intimidating. A server sets a bowl of cucumber soup in front of each guest.

But the bigger issue for me is being in the same room as Mrs. Jones and Madame. I try my best to avoid eye contact with Mrs. Jones during dinner, which isn't too hard since it seems Mrs. Jones is also avoiding me. But Madame, on the other hand, I study carefully. What did I experience at the other end of the light? Does Madame know about that place, too?

Dad always said that usually the most direct approach brings the most honest responses. So I take a deep breath and plunge forward.

"Do you believe in fairies, Madame?" I say.

Bella drops her spoon, causing soup to fly across the table and land on Mr. Parker's downturned mustache.

"Keira!" Mom gasps. "This is a formal dinner. Not a time for silly stories or jokes."

Madame lifts her eyebrows and stares at me in disbelief. "You cannot be serious, Miss Harding. Of course I do not believe in such nonsense."

"Do you own a clavichord here at this castle?" I continue, undaunted.

"I own nothing in this castle." Madame sets her spoon down. "I am merely the housekeeper. Now, if you would so kindly refrain from further interrogating, I would appreciate it."

"Keira!" Mom whispers harshly. "Stop being impolite and eat your soup!"

I bite my lip and focus on my puke-green soup. I know I haven't gone totally delusional because didn't both Chet and Bella see the light and then me disappear into it? There must be some clue I'm missing.

Chet raises his soup spoon to his mouth, blows, and takes a loud slurp. Grimacing, he spits it back into the bowl. Then when Madame and Mr. Parker aren't looking, he dumps the contents of the soup into the plant's soil behind him. He winks at me.

"Madame." Mrs. Jones dabs her lips clean of green soup. "You must give us the history of this castle."

Madame lifts her chin and stares evenly at each of us. As Madame's eyes pass over me, I can't stop the shudder that jerks through me. The silence lasts so long even Chet's dad allows his eyes to leave the steaming hot plate of lamb just served.

"Chenonceau has a history, indeed," Madame begins. "It was built as a fortified manor, but Thomas Bohier bought it, and Katherine Briconnet, his wife, transformed it into a lovely country castle."

"But I thought this was once one of the king's properties," Mrs. Jones probes.

Madame nods. "Indeed, King Francis the first loved the château so much that he forced the Bohier family to pay back taxes. As he knew, they couldn't pay such exorbitant fees, so Chenonceau became his, much to his delight."

"How terrible!" Bella says. "It's like he stole it from them."

"*Oh là là*," Madame says. "But then, who could resist such a beautiful place?"

"So it's still owned by royalty?" I say.

"*Non.*" Madame carefully slices a portion of her lamb and forks it with such grace that I cringe at my own peasant-like ways of stabbing my potatoes and slurping my soup. "It is owned by Monsieur Monteque, who bought it not so long ago. I do not listen to gossip, but rumor has it the previous owners lost it gambling."

"That's true." Mr. Jones points his fork at Madame. "You shouldn't listen to rumors."

"Where is the owner now?" Mrs. Jones asks.

"Monsieur is currently away on business."

"If I owned a castle," Bella says, waving her dinner roll like a scepter, "I'd never leave."

"Maybe he doesn't like the draftiness of a castle," Mr. Jones says quite pointedly at Madame. He's talking about last night. I shiver.

"*Non.*" Madame shoots a glare his way. "He cannot live here all of the time. Guests like you pay for the upkeep of such a place."

"I wonder how much *Girls' World* is paying for this little contest of theirs," Mom says. "Monsieur is sure to be making a large sum from this publicity."

"Oh, I bet they are paying him a lot of money," Bella says. "Cheryl showed me our dresses for the ball. They're designed by Chanel and completely divine."

"Forget the ball." Madame sits up in her chair. She slaps down her napkin and grits her teeth, losing all her pretense of civility. "How many times must I make this clear? There will be no ball."

"I don't understand what the problem with a ball is," Mom says.

"If you will excuse me." Madame pushes back her chair and strides out of the room in a flurry of black skirts.

After the servers whisk away the dinner plates, the cook parades in and plants lime sherbet in glass bowls in front of each of us so firmly that it's a miracle the glass doesn't break. The cook is still wearing her tall chef hat, though it now sags significantly to the side and her large white apron is smeared with food.

"Does Madame always get so aggravated?" Mrs. Jones asks the cook.

A hard, grim line forms on the cook's mouth. "You are brave, sleeping here zese nights."

"Brave?" I say.

"Dark zings are afoot in Chenonceau," she says. "Anozer of our servants went meessing last night. Be wary. All of you."

"We heard something about that, but assumed it was just a hoax." Mom sits straighter in her chair. "Whatever do you mean?"

"Don't say I did not warn you." Then the cook bustles out of the dining room without a backward glance.

"My!" Mrs. Jones says breathlessly, fanning herself. But oddly, her face is literally beaming. "That was exciting. Was it not?"

"Yeah, that was pretty cool." Chet nods and then turns to his dad. "Maybe this place isn't so bad."

But I, on the other hand, can't agree. The cook is right. There are dark secrets tucked away in the cobwebbed corners of this castle. And I, apparently, am one of them.

12

Sleuthing 101: The first task of fact-finding is to talk to anyone who was a witness to the scene of the crime.

SUNDAY (DIMANCHE), JUNE 13TH, 10:45 P.M.

"When are you going to turn that light out?" Bella complains from the other side of the bed, buried under a pile of covers.

While rummaging through the desk, I found an unused journal. Dust still caked its cover, so I figured Monsieur wouldn't mind me making notes in it. I decide to use it to record my latest findings like a true detective.

Joneses' Suspicious Behaviors:

1. *Mrs. Jones was hiding in the bushes.*
2. *She wore a hat and sunglasses as a disguise.*
3. *Lied about binoculars.*

Clues Discovered in the Joneses' Room:

1. *Hairnet*
2. *Suspicious books:* Manuel de l'immobilier *(which I found out translates to:* The Handbook to Real Estate) *and* The World's Scariest Ghost Stories
3. *Costume makeup*

I toss the journal aside and flip onto my stomach, staring at my suitcase, where my pen is tucked away safely inside. I can't help wondering if I used my special pen, would it give me the answers. A part of me wishes to jump off the bed and dig for the pen. But there's another part that's scared. Scared of the consequences. Why does writing have to be so wrong? It's not fair.

"What exactly did you see in the library when I was on the ladder?"

"Not again!" Bella groans.

I don't blame her for being annoyed. Since it rained all day and horseback riding was postponed to Wednesday, Madame gave us a very boring speech on French etiquette. Thankfully, that only lasted an hour. The rest of the day we spent trying out each door to see if the key Chet discovered fit any of them, and I rehashed my experience after flying off the ladder. Chet and Bella even climbed the ladder, waiting for something to happen, but nothing did. I'm beginning to wonder if I did hit my head and imagined it all.

"It was like a burst of white light and then you came rolling across the floor," Bella says. "Maybe Chet is right. Maybe it was a short circuit of electricity that caused the lights to get bright like that."

But what she said didn't make sense, because for me, it felt as if I had been gone for a long time.

"And then all that stuff the cook was saying with people going missing and darker things being afoot." I fidget with the bedspread. "What do you think she meant?"

"She's a loon. Go to sleep. I'm still jet-lagged and cranky."

"Fine," I huff, clicking off the light, only to stare into the dark canopy above.

It doesn't take Bella long before she's snoring away. My fingers ache. My pulse quickens. I slip out of bed, ever so quietly, and pad over to my suitcase. With shaking hands, I slip the pen out of its hiding place and hold it up to the moonlight, studying its gleam. I wait, squeeze it tight, and imagine that familiar rush of power streaming out of it.

But nothing happens.

I sigh and hunch over the pen. I wait for it to shine bright like it did before. But it keeps its silence. Maybe I did something wrong. Maybe it only works a certain number of times, like a genie released from its bottle. Who knows? I had hoped it would give me answers tonight.

Back in bed, I clutch the pen tightly in my hand, still not ready to return it to its hiding place. Shadows waltz across the walls as clouds weave in and out with the full moon. Outside, the wind howls and the river crashes against the castle walls. I tuck the covers up to my chin as if they would protect me. It's a long time before I finally fall asleep.

* * *

I wake with a jerk. At first I'm unsure what roused me, until I hear that stupid grandfather clock downstairs clanging away. Someone really needs to get that thing fixed. Beside me, Bella's body is flung out across the bed, all legs and arms. She's still snoring.

"This is why I don't do sleepovers anymore with you, Bella." I grunt. "The snoring."

Bella responds with a gurgling snort.

"At least you're sleeping well." I smile down at her while my stomach growls. "Well, Snow White, dream happily."

Haunting music drifts into our room. I sit up with a start, now fully awake. Every instinct in my body tells me to curl up under the covers and drift back into the haven of sleep. But I can't. After everything that has happened, my curiosity is at an all-time full alert. The clock reads 2:26 a.m. It's way too late to be prowling, but I've always believed it's best to face things head-on.

Like a header in soccer.

Careful not to wake Snow White, I slide out of bed and tiptoe across the floor, which is creaking and groaning with each step. After I tuck my pen back into its hiding place, I duck out into the hall. A shaft of light radiates from the stairway.

My hands clutch my pajama pants as I creep down the stairs. The cook's words haunt my thoughts: *Dark zings are afoot in Chenonceau.*

Is this what the cook had been talking about? Or maybe someone is just hanging out, relaxing to music at two in the morning.

Light spills out of the drawing room. Inside, the furniture is pushed against the walls and a crackling fire glows in the fireplace. The wood-beamed ceiling, along with the flower arrangements scattered about the room, gives the space a woodsy feel. But it's the old-fashioned piano against the far wall that catches my attention. Is that a clavichord?

The keys press down, creating the haunting melody that woke me. No one is playing it.

Do those things have AutoPlay?

A silvery figure dances past me, twirling in circles. I gasp as I recognize the dancing ghost. It's Gabrielle! The music grows louder, and as it does, laughter and chatter fill my ears. One by one, more ghosts cram into the room until the whole place is packed with dancers. Iridescent colors swirl amid their ghostlike paleness as if they're caught between the now and the past.

The firelight prickles, tugging at me. I grasp the doorframe to keep myself grounded. It's happening again!

But I can't resist its pull, and my body jerks into the room. The moment I enter, the colors solidify and the people about me no longer look like ghosts. Their skin takes on a warm glow, and the colors around me shine in rich patterns.

Gabrielle spies me. Her face breaks into a grin and she waves excitedly. But then her brow furrows when her eyes trail down my body, taking in my tank top and flannel pants.

She half dances, half runs to where I'm standing. Her golden gown sewn with gems and ribbons sparkles in the candlelight. A tiara perches on her head. She truly looks like a princess.

"Whatever art thou wearing?" Gabrielle says, aghast. "Thou lookest undeniably dreadful!"

"Yeah, it appears I underdressed. But you look gorgeous!"

Then Madame appears by the clavichord, holding a snowy white flower. Her face is as pale as death and her black skirts stand out in contrast to the ribbons of color streaming about the room. She beelines directly for Gabrielle.

Something is off. I try to warn Gabrielle, but my words jam in my throat. Madame sweeps to Gabrielle's side in seconds. With a flick of her wrist, Madame holds the flower out to Gabrielle.

"Take a whiff," Madame's voice is deep and airy.

"No!" I squeak.

But Gabrielle has already taken the flower. She smells it, and a wistful smile spreads over her face. But then the smile falters and she drops the flower. The petals scatter across the floor. Gabrielle slowly turns and, as if in a trance, begins to follow Madame through the crowd. A wrenching tug in my stomach tells me what's going to happen next.

I yell and make to run after Gabrielle, but a hand grabs on to the back of my shirt.

"Hot fire!" Chet yells. "This place is full of ghosts!"

His words shatter the magic.

Wind gushes toward me, blowing my hair back. I clamp my eyes shut against the dust billowing around me and dig my fingers into my palms, fighting against the wind so I won't crumple into a heap on the floor.

And then the gale stops. I open my eyes. The clavichord falls silent. The fireplace is dark and as cold as ashes. The ghosts have vanished.

"Man, did you see that?" Chet asks, eyes wide. His shirt is on backward. "The cook was right. Strange things *are* happening here. I'm so glad my dad brought me to this castle."

I smack Chet in the shoulder. "You ruined it! I was going to save her, but then you went and screamed and made it all disappear!"

"Chill out." Chet holds up his hands. "It's not like it's every day I see ghosts hanging around."

The swish of skirts and a beam of light skitters off the stairwell walls. Someone is coming!

"Quick!" I whisper in Chet's ear. "Hide!"

We scamper into the next room, but I don't know where to hide. Chet taps my shoulder and waves for me to follow him. He steps onto the edge of the couch, then up the side of a cupboard, and shinnies onto a window alcove. I take a deep breath and scurry after him.

Just as I squeeze in beside Chet, Madame glides into the room, her candle casting shadows in its wake. I hold my breath, the memory of Madame's flower scattering across the floor still vivid. When Madame finally does retreat, I clamp my hands together, hoping that will stop them from shaking.

Is it possible for Madame to be both a ghost and a real person? Where did Madame take Gabrielle?

"As fun as this is, why are we hiding from Madame again?" Chet says.

"I don't know." I rub the inside of my palm.

But the real question is, why did this all seem so similar to my own fairy tale?

13

Fact: In France before eating a meal, it is polite to say, "Bon appétit," which means "Good appetite."

MONDAY (LUNDI), JUNE 14TH, 9:00 A.M.

"Time to wake up!" a voice sings.

I bolt upright in bed, heart in my throat, expecting a ghost to be hovering at my bedside. Beside me, Bella grabs a pillow and throws it at the voice, all the while screaming.

"Oh, what a lovely, clear voice!"

Ugh. It's just Ms. Teppernat, clapping her hands in pure delight. She's wearing a bright yellow suit that could have passed for the sun itself, and her wedges click across the wooden floor as she paces at our bedside.

"How did you get in here?" I'm sure I locked the door last night.

"Madame gave us a key when I asked for it," Ms. Teppernat says.

"Threatened is more like it," Cheryl mutters under her breath as she steps into the room.

"It may be raining outside, but that is no cause for alarm," Ms. Teppernat says. "Because we switched the boating trip already with our cooking session, as is noted in your schedule. Come along, girls. Find those beautiful smiles and hop out of bed!"

Bella leaps out of bed with a squeal, but I roll over and groan into my pillow. Until I remember the cook's words. She warned us about dark things afoot in the castle. I bet she knows more about what's going on here than she's letting on. This will be the perfect opportunity to talk to her.

"Today you will be fashioned after the fairy tale of Snow White," Cheryl explains through a mouthful of pins as she rolls in a cart full of dresses and outfits. All the colors in the rack are blues, yellows, and reds.

"Snow White?" I sag back into the pillows. "We're doing another photo shoot? I don't think I can handle that."

"Never fear!" Ms. Teppernat says brightly. "As soon as we're finished, you're free to spend the rest of the day as you please."

"Just as long as I don't have to sing and have birds dance on my head," I say.

Ms. Teppernat pats me on the cheek. "You are so funny!"

Bella oohs over each dress as she flips through them on the cart. "How are we supposed to decide which outfit to wear? They're all so lovely."

I make myself get out of bed and look through the dresses. I pluck a blue one and hold it up against me.

"That's the perfect color for you," Bella says. "Speaking of perfect colors, have you seen my purple sundress? I looked everywhere for it yesterday."

"Nope." I twirl around with my dress. "Maybe it's hanging out with my missing music player. I went to charge it last night but couldn't find it."

"Maybe it's the ghost," Cheryl says nervously. "The townsfolk say the castle is haunted."

After getting dressed, even I have to admit how fun dressing up is. I end up choosing the royal-blue sleeveless dress and drape a heart pendant necklace around my neck. Then Bella helps me pick out a yellow cardigan to complete my outfit.

The most difficult part ends up being the red strappy wedges Cheryl gives me. I practice walking in them, but I end up doing more wobbling than walking.

"Don't worry about the shoes," Bella says. "Because you look positively divine. The dress totally brings out the blue in your eyes."

Then for herself, she chooses a pleated yellow skirt that flares out at her hips, and a blue cardigan sweater that accents her brown skin.

"Wow," I tell Bella. "You definitely have the eye for style. You look as perfect as a princess."

"It's a modern version of Snow White," Bella explains, beaming at my compliment.

As we head downstairs, I have a hard time focusing on Ms. Teppernat's instructions. A camera crew joins us on the first floor, and Mom rushes to my side. Her hair is puffed out as if she didn't sleep a wink.

"Did you notice anything unusual last night?" Mom clenches a list in her hand.

"Um—no." I rub my palm, unsure how to explain the dancing ghost or if I even wanted to. Knowing Mom, she'll freak out at the first hint of something that isn't fact-driven.

"That's good," Mom says absentmindedly. "Well, I suppose I should stop worrying, then. Oh! And I made a list of different types of foods that the French eat. Did you know that they have over three hundred and sixty-five types of cheese?"

"Great," I murmur. "We can eat a new one every day of the year."

As soon as we enter the basement, I scope the area for Madame and hope she stays clear of the photo shoot. An image of her pops into my head. She's wearing a black pointed hat and emerges from a burst of smoke and white flowers.

The smell of fresh baked bread floats down the hallway, and my stomach rumbles. I wish we got to have breakfast first. Ms. Teppernat leads us to the sound of clanging pots, to a room at the end of the hall. It's there that we find the cook, chopping onions and peppers. A tabloid magazine lies open next to her.

"*Oh là là!*" the cook says, pausing mid-stroke. "So many cameras."

"Don't be ridiculous," Ms. Teppernat responds. "It's just two. Now shall we get started?"

While Ms. Teppernat barks out orders, Bella and I drool over the mound of baguettes and croissants. Fortunately, Ms. Teppernat is too busy setting up the scene to notice Bella and me grab a croissant each and stuff them into our mouths.

"You like, huh?" the cook says, a gleam in her eye. "Do not worry. My leeps are silent."

"Thanks," I say, my mouth full.

"So for this photo session," Ms. Teppernat says once the crew is ready, "you'll be cooking French toast soufflé. It's going to be *so* much fun!"

"Of course!" Mom refers to her list. "*Pain perdu*, which means 'lost bread' in English."

Cook takes over the instructions from there, showing us how to dip the bread into an egg batter, fry it on the stove, which looks like it belongs in the eighteen hundreds, and sprinkle cinnamon and powdered sugar over the top. The camera crew videos and snaps so many pictures I'm not sure what they'll do with them all.

Beside us, Mom takes copious notes, determined that we'll re-create the recipe at home. "How many teaspoons of sugar did you sprinkle on top?" Mom asks the cook.

"As much as needed," the cook says vaguely. "A dusting, yes?"

"But how much is that precisely? One teaspoon? Two?"

While Mom debates with the cook, a dark-haired head bobs along the back wall behind the pile of potatoes and pots.

Then the head pops up, revealing Chet and his signature mischievous smile.

He puts one finger to his lips, then creeps behind the cameramen and snags four chocolate croissants before slipping back behind the counter. Seeing Chet reminds me once again of last night, and my stomach twists. I set down my plate, determined to get to the bottom of things.

Bella is so engrossed in a conversation with Cheryl about what to order to go with her designs for the ball that I decide this is the perfect moment to ask.

"What did you mean last night," I say, sidling next to the cook as everyone begins to head out, "when you said the castle was haunted?"

The cook stops slicing, holding her knife frozen in the air. "Haunted, *chérie*? I never used such word."

"Well, you said something like that. Why work here if there are dark things happening? With this amazing cooking, you could work at any posh restaurant."

The cook snorts. "Not for zee euro I get."

"You're well paid?" I press.

"Monsieur pays double anyone else." She shrugs and resumes her chopping. "So I work."

"So it's like hazard pay."

"I do not know what you mean." The cook waves her knife around, scrunching her nose. "You are a nice girl. I would hateet eef you deesappear."

"Um, thanks. I think." I smile uneasily, all the while keeping a sharp eye on the swooping knife. "Why would I disappear?"

"You must go before *le vendredi*."

"Go before Friday? Why?"

"At *Château de Chenonceau*, we call *le vendredi* 'la nuit de la mort.'" The cook leans her bulk over the counter. Her breath smells like onions. "No one works on zat night. Zat ees why you must leave."

"*La nuit de la mort?*" Chet peeks up from behind the potatoes. "That means Friday is the Night of Death."

"Why are you in my kitchen?" The cook jams her fist onto her hip, frowning.

"I may have gotten a little hungry," Chet says sheepishly.

"Ah! So *you* are zee kitchen zief."

"Guilty. But your chocolate croissants are *so* good."

This makes the cook purse her lips and lift her hand proudly. "*Oui*, zey are zee best."

"How do you know it means Night of Death?" I ask Chet.

"Being from Quebec means I'd be booted out if I didn't speak a little French," Chet says.

The basement staircase creaks, and I realize everyone has left except Chet and me. The kitchen suddenly doesn't feel quite as warm and friendly.

"Cook!" Madame's voice vibrates down the hall, calling for the cook. "*Nous devons parler!*"

"Why does Madame want to talk to you?" Chet asks.

"*Allez!*" the cook says. "Madame must not know we speak."

"Why?" I say.

The cook doesn't bother answering. Instead, she shoves Chet and me into a back corner and lifts a fire poker next to the fireplace. Alarmed, I start backing away, but the poker never comes out of its mooring. Instead, the stone wall behind the fireplace moves inward just enough for a person to squeeze through, revealing a tiny room strung with cobwebs and full of dust balls.

"Hurry!" The cook shoos us inside. "Hide!"

My eyes widen. What is this place?

*Fact: Within the pyramids, the ancient Egyptians built
secret rooms underneath the main passages as decoy
rooms to mislead tomb raiders.*

Jumping into a dark and cobweb-ridden hideout isn't on my
to-do list. In fact, the garbage heap in the corner of the kitchen
looks more inviting than this secret room.

"A secret passageway!" Chet peers nervously into the narrow opening. "You sure it's safe?"

"I don't know what the problem is," I say, deciding I'm
most definitely not going in there. "Why can't we just talk to
Madame?"

Without warning, the cook's strong arms grab hold of
Chet and me and shove us inside the secret opening. The wall
clamps back into place, nearly severing my fingers.

Blackness and sudden silence blanket me in terror that only
complete darkness can give. I grope the void until my hands
smack Chet's nose.

"Hey!" Chet says. "Stop mangling me."

"I wasn't mangling you!" I huff and try to collect my
thoughts. Mom always said it's best to stay calm and focused.
But then, I'm sure she's never been in this situation. "We need
to deal with this calmly by taking one step at a time."

"Sure, as long as step one means you stop elbowing me."

I paw at the blackness, cringing at the thought that there might be gross creatures crawling around or dangling from the ceiling. "I'm sure the cook wouldn't have locked us in here without a flashlight or a way to get out."

My fingers touch something hard and smooth. *A flashlight!* I seize it, but the object moves. Tiny feet patter up my arm.

"It's a bug!" I scream, trying to brush it off. "Watch out!"

My arm smacks into Chet. Something thumps at my feet.

"Ow!" he says.

A light tapping sound skitters across the floor. Then silence. I release a long breath.

"It's gone now," I say. "That's good, right?"

"Don't worry about me," Chet groans from the floor. "I'm fine."

"Oh, sorry." I grope through the darkness until I grasp Chet's hand and help him up. "You okay? Creepy-crawly things and I don't get along well."

"Really? I would never have guessed. Just no more screaming today. My ears are still ringing."

"How long do you think we have to wait here until the cook opens the door?" I say. "She can't expect us to hang out here all day."

"Check this out. I think this is a message or something."

White circles no bigger than my fingernail are inlaid in the stone. They glow ever so slightly in the darkness.

"What are they?" I say. "How are they glowing?"

"I don't know, but look, there's a whole line of them."

"It's like a path!"

We aren't in a hidden room. We're in a secret passageway!

But with that thought comes the realization that I've been in a secret passageway before in this castle. When I followed Gabrielle and was chased by something horrible.

As we follow the white specks, a sick dread fills me. Hadn't the princess in my fairy tale escaped the evil stepsister in a dark, twisted tunnel lit by gems? And if so, did that mean that the things I experienced hadn't been dreams but real events somehow connected to my fairy tale?

The similarities of this moment and my fairy tale terrify me.

I shuffle along behind Chet until the circles lead us to a staircase, so narrow and steep it could almost pass for a ladder. The line of white specks ends abruptly at the top of the stairs, on the ceiling.

"Here goes," Chet says as he scales the stairs. At the top, he searches the ceiling with his hands. "There's got to be some way out. Otherwise, why would the builders go to such trouble to build this staircase?"

He pushes on the ceiling and then on the wall beside him. Nothing happens.

"Stupid wall." He kicks at the stone and as he does, one of the rocks thrusts inward. The wall behind him slides away and Chet tumbles out of my sight. Light floods the passageway.

"Chet!" I clamber after him.

When I reach the top, I realize Chet has discovered the exit of the passageway. I duck through the opening under the low stone ceiling, scramble over some logs, and stumble out into the library. Dusty and sooty.

I've just tumbled out of a fireplace.

*   *   *

Before I can process everything, the back of the fireplace slides closed. If I hadn't stumbled through it, I never would've guessed it's an entrance to a secret passageway from the outside. That's two fireplaces in this castle which lead to secret passageways. That is, if the one the other night hadn't been a dream.

"There you are!" Bella says, sauntering into the room, sketchbook in hand. She raises her eyebrows, looking at Chet and me as if we'd grown unicorn horns or something.

"Why are you staring at the fireplace?" she says. "And what happened to your dress?"

Bella is so never going to believe me. "We just came from behind it," I say.

She giggles. "You two need to get out more."

"No. Seriously," Chet says. "It's a secret tunnel."

"Really? So it's like an enchanted castle?" Bella says with a look of *Sure, I'll play along with your little game.* But then she frowns and tugs at my hair. "Did you know you have cobwebs in your hair?"

"Ugh!" Pulling my hair band out, I throw my head upside down and brush out my hair. If there are cobwebs, then there might've been spiders down there, too. For once, I'm glad it was dark. When I look back up, Bella is on her knees next to Chet, peeking up the chimney shaft.

"More like haunted if you ask me," Chet mutters.

"Haunted?" Bella says.

"Yep," Chet says. "This morning I went looking for my rock climbing shoes. But they're missing."

"You think a ghost took them?" Bella says.

"I haven't had a chance to talk to you about it all," I tell Bella. "But last night—" I bite my lip. Just saying what I saw hurtles a shiver down my arms.

"We saw a bunch of ghosts," Chet says for me, plopping down on one of the couches. "And then Madame showed up and we hid from her."

"What do you mean you saw ghosts?" Bella says.

I glance at the library ladder that sent me plunging into what I'm beginning to think is my fairy-tale world. "I suppose I should explain everything from the beginning."

So I tell them everything that has happened to me so far. Chet whistles and shakes his head, but Bella shoots me a skeptical look.

"Okaaay." She sets down her sketchbook. "Are you guys playing a game on me? Because if you are, you got me. Very funny. Ha-ha-ha."

"But we're not joking," Chet says. "There really were ghosts, and Madame was one of them. And we really found a secret passageway. I just don't know how to open it from this side."

"Do you understand how ridiculous you sound?" she says.

"That's not even the craziest part, though," I say, and bury my head in my hands. "Remember when I wrote that fairy tale for the contest? Well, everything that has happened so far is just like my fairy tale. The castle is the same, there is a princess and an evil stepsister. And get this: My main character's name is Gabrielle, just like the ghost."

"The ghost has a name? You've talked to it?" Bella says. "Maybe your brain is just trying to imagine your story."

"So what happens to Gabrielle in your story?" Chet asks.

"She vanishes," I say. "On the night of the ball."

"And we're having a ball this Friday," Chet says in a hushed voice. *"La nuit de la mort."*

*Sleuthing 101: The best way to tell if someone is
lying is to find changes in their story.*

"You can't be serious," Bella says. "I'm so not falling for this
story. Keira, you know I adore you, but this is going too far."

"I am totally in," Chet says. "This is the coolest adventure
I've had maybe in my life."

"Bella," I say. "You have to believe me. I don't know what's
going on, but maybe Madame is right. Maybe we shouldn't
have the ball on Friday. Or maybe we should just go home."

"You know I can't do that. Not after all the planning that
I've put into this ball. It's going to be the most magical night.
Ms. Teppernat let me order whatever decorations I wanted.
We can't just cancel this because of you two and your games."

"I'm not playing games, Bella," I say. "Let's try out the
ladder again and see what happens. Maybe it will work this
time and you'll believe me."

"Fine." Bella stalks over to the ladder and steps onto it.
"I will."

I grip the sides of the desk, waiting for Bella to feel something. But she turns and shrugs her shoulders. Meanwhile,
Chet begins pulling all the fireplace tools and pushing on the
different bricks along the edges.

"I don't feel anything, Keira," Bella says. "Now will you
please stop goofing off and try to not ruin this ball for me?"

"But I know it happened!" Now it's my turn to touch the ladder, hoping for the spark to ignite this time. For it to glisten in a frost of white.

But it doesn't.

I look to Chet for support. He clears his throat awkwardly and then pulls out a small rope from his pocket and starts twisting it into a knot.

"I know what I saw, Bells," I say. "You have to believe me."

"Why don't you talk to Chet about it all since you two are such good friends now," Bella says and storms out of the library.

*　*　*

I race into the hall, trying to catch up with her, just as the butler opens the front door for Ms. Teppernat. Her cell phone is pressed to her ear, an umbrella tucked under her arm.

"Everything is in place," Ms. Teppernat is saying. "I put my foot down about Friday, too."

A creaking from the stairwell catches my attention. A flash of white hair disappears behind the wall. Mrs. Jones caught spying again.

"Of course. Uh-huh," Ms. Teppernat says into her cell.

It's time to take matters into my own hands. I need to warn Ms. Teppernat of my fears about the ball being on Friday. I breathe in deeply and then march over to the yellow-dressed dragon.

"Ms. Teppernat," I say.

Ms. Teppernat freezes in the hallway. "Well, that's your choice, isn't it?" Ms. Teppernat tells her caller. "Just a moment, the girl is here."

Ms. Teppernat's gaze focuses on me. "What?"

I jerk back, hesitating. All of Ms. Teppernat's sugary words and smiles have vanished.

"I don't have all day." Ms. Teppernat taps her foot.

I lick my lips. "There's something about the castle you should know."

She cocks her head and narrows her eyes.

"I think the castle is haunted. There's a ghost that comes out at night and I think the ghost is the one who took the maid and is planning on taking more people."

Ms. Teppernat straightens and sighs. She brings her cell back to her ear and says, "She knows."

Daily Fact-Seeker Fact of the Day: A common belief for why ghosts exist is that the ghost has unfinished business, which we have proclaimed as complete nonsense.

"Excuse me?" I'm so shocked by her response that I'm at a loss for words.

Ms. Teppernat ends her call, and her eyes search the hallway. "Ah! Here's my little darling! Can't leave without it, now can I?" She snatches up her silver glitter purse lying on the hall table and slips her phone inside.

"I know this may be hard to swallow." She puckers her red lips dramatically. "But Chenonceau has a long history of supposed ghost sightings. It's completely normal in these parts, and despite what the locals say, the château is perfectly safe. This ball on Friday is going to prove to the world that Chenonceau is the most magical place on earth. Not some haunted ghost playground."

"But what about the maid?"

"Oh, her?" Ms. Teppernat scoffs. "Apparently, she quit. Couldn't stand Madame DuPont. Who could blame the poor girl? But never fear. We will make sure you get a new maid."

"I don't want a maid," I say. "I want to make sure everyone is safe."

"Don't worry yourself over it," Ms. Teppernat says gaily.

"Just get rested for a big day of boating tomorrow! The schedule must continue!"

Ms. Teppernat snaps open her umbrella and waltzes out into the rain, not once looking back.

Tuesday (Mardi), June 15th

It rains the next day as well, pattering against the windowpanes and filling the river Cher, so Ms. Teppernat reschedules the boating trip to Friday. As the evening draws in, the rain stops, leaving behind a mist that swirls through the forest and trickles across the castle lawn and gardens like a thick winter blanket.

Bella went to the local florist with Cheryl to choose the flower arrangements for the ball, leaving me alone to prowl the halls in search of Mom. Even though it isn't a large château, there are plenty of nooks and crannies to hide away in. Finally, I find her strolling from portrait to portrait in the ballroom. I've been avoiding this long stretch of the castle ever since I saw the eyes move in the picture frame.

"Hey, Mom," I say. "I have a question for you."

"Why, of course. I was just making a genealogical list of the family history. It's all so fascinating."

"Do you believe in ghosts?"

"What? Of course not!" Her voice nearly screeches, and then her eyes narrow suspiciously. "There is no factual evidence that claims they are real. Why are you asking?"

"I know this sounds crazy, but I think this castle is haunted by ghosts." I cringe, waiting for her to explode over the irrationality of my theory.

"Keira, you need to stop with the fairy tales and stories. It just isn't healthy."

"I'm serious, Mom! Even Ms. Teppernat says that this part of France is known for having ghosts. She acted like it was common knowledge."

Mom gives me a hard look, tapping her pencil on the pad of paper. "Common knowledge, huh? Well, as long as it doesn't affect us, then we shouldn't have to worry."

I swallow hard. A part of me is desperate to tell her that the ghost *is* affecting me, that I *am* being pulled into the ghost's world, and that it *is* eerily connected to the very same fairy tale I wrote.

But if I do, Mom will completely flip out and then watch me like a hawk until the day I die. Besides, Mom does have a point. It isn't like the ghost is affecting anyone. No one is getting hurt. According to Ms. Teppernat, the maid who we thought disappeared quit because of Madame, the Wicked Witch of the West.

"It looks like we have a reprieve from the rain," Mom says. "How about we head to town for a little shopping and dinner? We'll wait until Bella gets back, and the three of us will get out and see some of France while we're here."

"Getting out of here sounds great," I say as I eye the portraits, half expecting one of them to move.

*　　*　　*

Bella chooses to stay behind to work with Cheryl on the arrangements for the ball, so Pierre drives Mom and me into the neighboring village of Chenonceaux. The narrow road is canopied with large oaks. Vineyards spread out on either side, their leaves a bright green in the fading light.

Pierre drops us off on the side of the cobblestone street in the center of the village. Ivy clings to the white stone buildings. Lanterns glow in the early evening, giving the rain-slick sidewalks a warm, welcoming feel. The air smells of flowers and freshly baked bread, which I decide is the most magical combination.

The tiny village is packed with gabled windows and cute doors. Music strikes up ahead in the square, and restaurant owners have opened their doors to lure shoppers with dinner scents.

Mom and I stroll down the street, taking in the quaintness and beauty until we find the shopper's paradise. A boutique crammed with clothing, postcards, books on castles, and other castle knickknacks.

"So tell me a little about these ghosts," Mom says as she inspects the long strands of necklaces by the counter. "What makes you think they're real?"

I study her in surprise. Normally, she's not receptive to chat about these kinds of topics, but tonight she actually sounds rational and calm. The pressure of this secret has been building up inside me. Maybe she can help me.

"I think I saw one." I pick through the postcards on the rack until I find one Dad will like. But really all I can focus on is my magical pen tucked away in my suitcase. Tonight I need to try it out again. It's helped me before, maybe it can help me again. "Remember that first night in the hallway?"

"That's right. It was the night with all of the wind from the storm." Mom abandons the necklaces, suddenly concentrating on me. I fidget under her intense gaze. "But you don't believe it had anything to do with that storm, do you?"

"No. Well, maybe. And here's the strangest part." I take a deep breath because my throat pinches so tight. "The things I keep seeing remind me a lot of the fairy tale I wrote."

"Keira." She wrings her hands and sags into the chair by the changing room. "You—oh, never mind."

"What?"

"It's nothing. Just the past creeping up on me."

"What do you mean?"

"Do you remember that empty box that I thought the burglars had taken something from?" I nod. "It had a pen in it. A very special pen."

"Really?" I play with a sundress hanging on the rack so Mom won't see my face. I'm sure I look guilty. Mom eyes me suspiciously.

"Oh, Keira! Tell me you didn't use that pen to write your fairy tale."

"No!" I say before I can stop the lie from slipping out.

The panic leaves her face as she tilts her head back and closes her eyes. Guilt pokes me that I lied to my mom again. Still, a thousand alarms ring in my head. Why did she suspect I used that pen to write the story? Was it a coincidence?

"Good. I'm glad." She visibly shivers. "I have to admit that I was skeptical, considering you won a contest with such an amazing prize."

"You don't think I am a good enough writer to win this contest on my own?" I say. Suddenly, tears form in my eyes. I don't even know why I'm crying. I just know that I'm on the most magical trip of my life and everything feels wrong. "That's what this is all about, isn't it? Or maybe it's not that you don't believe I'm talented, but you don't want me to be successful."

"It's not that, sweetie. You are incredibly talented. I don't think writing should be a part of your—"

I can't listen to another word because I know this speech by heart. I race out the door and storm down the street. But then my steps slow as a new thought hits me. What if Mom is right? That I didn't win because of my talent. That I won because of a magical pen.

What if that pen truly is magical? Then maybe all the ghosts and fairies and crazy things I have been seeing are actually connected to the pen in some way.

Which is either pretty cool or pretty horrible.

"Keira!" Panting, my mom is running down the sidewalk to catch up with me. She draws me into a big hug. "Don't ever run away like that again! I didn't know where you went."

I wrap my arms around her. It has been a long time since we hugged like this. It's annoying to have her be over-the-top protective and controlling, but at least I know she cares.

"Come on," Mom says. "Let's go have some dinner."

We start down the sidewalk, when across the street in an Internet café, I spot Chet and his dad sitting at computers along the glass wall.

"Is that Chet and his dad?" I say.

"Well! I think you're right."

"Come on, let's surprise them."

But midway across the street, a car zooms around the corner, nearly running us over.

"Watch out, Mom!" I grab her arm and practically throw her onto the sidewalk. We tumble across the pavement as tires screech to a stop. The car bumper has missed my leg by inches.

"Gracious!" Mom brushes off the gravel from her pants. "You saved our lives! I never saw the car coming."

"It nearly ran us over."

I turn to study the car. The driver whips her long wavy light brown hair to lock eyes with me. I know those eyes! Sure, the hair color is different and her skin doesn't look so powdery white or wrinkled, but I'd know that face anywhere.

Mrs. Jones.

The driver pushes on a pair of sunglasses, even though the sun has set, and slams on the gas, screeching down the street.

"I think that was Mrs. Jones." I place my hand over my chest, still remembering the heat of the engine.

Mom laughs, a bit shaken. "That was definitely not Mrs. Jones, sweetie. But you do have an active imagination, I'll give you that."

* * *

We enter the Internet café to find Chet and his dad fighting.

"How could you do that, Dad?" I hear Chet saying. "They trust us. I was finally starting to make friends."

"You're making a bigger deal of it than it is," Mr. Parker says.

Mom and I hover off to the side until Mr. Parker spots us and literally jumps out of his chair like he's seen a ghost.

"Wow." He chuckles nervously while running his hands over his hair as if he's making sure the perfect swoop is still intact. "You two got me there. Didn't even hear you sneak up."

"Sorry, but Chet deserves payback for all the times he's snuck up on me," I say. Then I tell them how we were nearly run over by a woman who looked a lot like Mrs. Jones.

"That's far out," Chet says. "I've never had to dodge an out-of-control driver or save anyone's life. I'm going to have to add it to my list of Cool Things to Do."

"But isn't Mrs. Jones elderly?" Mr. Parker says. "There's no way she'd be racing around town, running people over."

"That's the thing," I say. "I think Mrs. Jones is dressing up in disguise."

"Sounds pretty far-fetched to me," Mr. Parker says.

"Keira does have an active imagination when it comes to people, but she just saved our lives, so I'm proud of my brave girl." Mom gives me a side-squeeze and then launches into an account of interesting city facts to Mr. Parker. I tune them out and begin reading the email Mr. Parker had been writing on his screen. It isn't my fault; I'd been training my whole life to be a detective.

The girl is the prime suspect. Ghosts have been cited. Still need—

Before I can read more, Mr. Parker turns and clicks SEND. The email vanishes into cyberspace.

But I'd seen enough to know that Chet's dad may be holding a few secrets of his own.

*Fact: A horse's teeth take up more space in its head
than its brain does.*

WEDNESDAY (MERCREDI), JUNE 16TH

By the time I finish dressing the next morning, I could pass for a true equestrian. Bella and I head to the stables, wearing crisp riding habits Cheryl has fitted us in, complete with tight tan breeches, a form-fitting black shirt, boots that pull up to the knees, and even a whip and hat.

"I've never ridden a horse before." I fidget with my whip and wonder what I'm supposed to do with it.

"I have a couple of times at summer camp," Bella says. "It's super easy. I'm sure you'll ace it."

"I hope you're right. You've got to admit that riding horses at a castle has got to be one of the most magical things ever."

"Absolutely!" Bella say. "I wish we were here for two weeks instead of one."

It's also a bit of a relief to leave behind the ghosts and crazy hallucinations from the castle and focus on having fun with Bella. As we step into the stable area, my steps falter when I find Chet sitting on one of the posts, tying a knot, wearing jeans and a hockey shirt.

"Are you going riding, too?" I say.

"I'm hoping they'll let me," Chet says.

I'm not sure how I feel about Chet after seeing the email his dad wrote. Can I trust him? What did that email mean, anyway? Normally, I'd have told Bella about my suspicions, but every time I bring it up, I stop, remembering her reaction when she thought Chet and I were playing a joke on her with the castle being haunted. Besides, maybe that email wasn't a big deal. Maybe it was my overactive brain making something out of nothing.

"Keira!" Ms. Teppernat parades in with her film crew entourage. Today she's wearing tight jeans and a sequined green shirt that matches her green eyes. "Why are you not on your horse yet?"

"You're filming us riding, too?" I suppress a groan, not wanting everyone to see how scared I am of horses. "What if I fall off the horse and look like a complete idiot?"

"Don't be so morbid," Bella says. "Think of it as one more thing to add to our amazing adventures here."

But Ms. Teppernat doesn't bother with an explanation. "Let's get moving before the rain starts, everyone. Chop-chop!"

"Can I ride, too?" Chet asks.

"Absolutely not!" But then Ms. Teppernat scrutinizes Chet, tapping her fingers on her red lips. "Hmm. I suppose you could be useful. But you'll have to sign a waiver."

"Hot fire!" Chet punches the air. "Sign me up."

"Cheryl!" Ms. Teppernat says. "Get the boy a new shirt. That jersey is positively disgusting."

"Hey!" Chet jumps off his post. "You have a problem with the Montreal Canadiens, the best team ever?"

But Ms. Teppernat simply waves her hand to him in dismissal and moves on, barking out instructions to the camera crew. Meanwhile, Andre the stableman gives the horses a final check and leads them by the reins outside. I sidle against the wooden fence, swallowing down my fear of having to sit on top of the massive beast. One of my friends at school used to ride until she was thrown off her horse and broke her arm.

Chet saunters over to me, jamming his hands in his pockets. "You sure left quickly last night," he says. "You upset about something I said?"

I shrug my shoulders, acting like nothing is bothering me, though the email and his argument with his dad are still fresh in my mind. But I don't really want to talk about last night right now. All I want is to survive this photo shoot.

"Got any tips on how to ride a horse?" I ask him instead.

"You've never ridden?" Chet acts like everyone on the planet rides horses.

"Well, other than jumping on my horse and riding to school and the grocery store," I say sarcastically. "No, I haven't. And I'm slightly terrified of horses."

Ms. Teppernat must have overheard us, because she throws up her hands. "What? Did you hear that, Cheryl? She's never ridden. Someone give her a lesson. And quick!"

"I'll teach her," Chet offers. Then he turns to me with a grin. "It's not hard to learn the basics."

The thought of Chet teaching me how to ride doesn't sit well with me. But I clip on my riding helmet, determined to not let my fears stop me. My horse, whose name is Felipe, according to the stable master, whips his mane and paws at the ground. He's ready to hit the trail. Meanwhile, Bella has already mounted her horse and is circling the yard.

How am I supposed to get on this Giganter? I inch forward and gingerly brush my hand over Felipe's smooth brown hair. It feels like warm velvet, but full of life and energy.

"It's really easy." Chet comes to my side, grabs the reins and slaps the saddle with his palm. "Just step into the stirrup and swing your other leg over the horse."

I grimace. "Easy for you maybe."

The horse shifts and grunts as I belly onto its back. I clutch the saddle, but from this position I can't manage to swing my leg over for anything. I shift, gritting my teeth and taking a deep breath, telling myself that I can do this.

"So how do I swing my leg over?"

Chet laughs. "Might be hard to do in that position."

As if sensing my discomfort, Felipe tosses his head and steps forward. Andre calls out "Whoa," but I can't control my body. I lose my grip and slide facedown the other side of the horse. My head almost hits the ground, but I manage to grab the edge of the saddle. The tip of my braid brushes the dirt below me.

"Ahhh!" I cry as my head dangles next to the stirrup. My boots stick straight into the air. Then a terrible thing happens. My grip on the saddle begins to slip.

"Somebody save Keira!" Bella yells, which only makes things worse, because her horse bucks at the sudden noise.

Chet dives and grabs my shoulders seconds before my head hits the ground. We sprawl into the dirt, and I land smack on top of him.

"Don't let her outfit get dusty!" Cheryl says.

"Got that covered," Chet says with a groan.

"I couldn't bear it if you died." Bella slides off her horse and runs to me. She helps me to my feet.

"She's not going to die." Chet rolls his eyes.

"This was a bad idea," Ms. Teppernat says. "Maybe we should call this excursion off."

"No." I march back over to my horse. "I'm going to do this."

Finally, after two more tries, I find myself sitting tall and triumphant atop Felipe. Andre takes my reins and leads my horse to stand in front of the castle, next to Chet and Bella on their horses. The cameras flash for each pose.

"Wonderful!" Ms. Teppernat calls out. "Now let's take them past the gardens into the forest."

My heart skips a beat when I realize I'm actually going to ride a horse, not just sit on top of one. Andre lets go of my horse and jumps into the back of one of the two golf carts.

"Where are you going?" I ask him, but he's already buzzing ahead on his cart. I fidget with the reins, unsure how to even hold them. "How do I make this horse go?"

"These horses are trained English-style," Chet says. "Pull the left rein toward you, and the horse will turn left. Pull the right one, and he'll turn right."

"That sounds easy enough." I try it. It works! I flash Chet a grateful smile. "Where did you learn to ride?"

"My uncle's place is just outside of Newport. He's got a bunch of horses. I stay with him most of the time when my mom and dad are traveling. This is the first time I've actually gotten to go with my dad on a trip."

The horses' shoes clip on the stone path, which snakes through the gardens, winding its way toward the forest ahead. A light breeze blows in from across the river and sunlight sparkles on the water.

The camera crew is already in position ahead of us, snapping away. Ms. Teppernat waves her cell phone to get our attention. Sensing that isn't working, she starts yelling something.

"What's she saying?" I squint, trying to read her lips.

"No clue," Chet says.

"I think she's saying 'time to stop.'" Bella cranes her head to the side. "Or is she saying 'time to trot'?"

"Trot?"

As soon as I say "trot," Felipe takes off at a brisk pace. Frantic, I grapple with the reins, bobbing and jiggling all over my saddle as though I'm in a bouncy house. The path becomes a dirt trail that stretches into the forest. Tall oak trees twist into a gnarled nest above, shutting out the sun. It's as if I've stepped into Hansel and Gretel's woods.

"Slow down!" Chet yells from behind me.

"Pull back on the reins!" Bella says.

I yank back, but instead of slowing down, my actions seem to propel Felipe faster. He bucks and then canters off at full speed as if he knows I'm not in control. Soon I'm galloping down the forest path, wind lashing across my face. Somehow I've lost my grip on the reigns so now I'm holding onto the saddle horn for my life. I don't think anything could get worse until a plop of water hits the top of my helmet. And then another.

"Perfect." I grumble as misty air rushes past my face. "It's raining!"

I bop up and down so hard on the saddle I bet I'm going to get bruises. Then it's as if the clouds open up and the giant from *Jack and the Beanstalk* has dumped a giant barrel of water on me.

Blinded by the rain and the foggy forest, I barely see the tree bough looming ahead. I sink below the horse's neck to prepare to go under the bough. It just skims the top of my helmet. I'm saved.

Except I don't take into account the fallen log that comes after the bough. The horse leaps. He flies through the air— and then *bam!*—hits the other side of the path, splashing into a puddle. My fingers slip from the saddle horn, and my body hurdles off the horse. I hit the ground with a hard thud, before face-planting in the mud.

Ugh! My chest hurts so bad, and I can't breathe! I gasp for air as I lie flat in a puddle, rain splattering on my face. And then my breathing resumes.

Inhale, exhale, inhale, exhale.

I lift my head just in time to watch my horse canter away around a corner in the path, mud splattering in its wake. *Thank you very much, Felipe.*

Mud cakes my body as I crawl out of the puddle. A nearby tree offers me protection, so I huddle beneath it. I close my eyes, telling myself to take a few minutes to recover before heading back to the castle.

In the distance, the boom of a gong cuts through the air. My eyes pop open. That can't be the castle's grandfather clock striking the turn of the hour. That's impossible! The mist swirls up along the path, picking up speed and thickness until the entire forest is draped in it as if the mist is a living thing. The air cools and I shiver, rubbing my arms up and down to try to keep away the chill as the grandfather clock keeps tolling. A warning.

Saying, *Run! Run! Run!* with each clang.

Then out of the mist, a horse appears. At first I think it's Felipe. But the fog shifts, and I realize it's something different entirely.

The horse's body is sleek and muscular, as if used to running in the wild. The mane consists of a tangle of black curls that drape along its body like waves cascading onto the beach. Bright and wild eyes assess me huddled in the cold, wet mud.

But what takes my breath away is the glittering emerald horn jutting from its forehead and the long wings that beat ever so slightly, stirring up a breeze. This is no ordinary horse.

It is Pegasus.

*Fact: Horses don't have wings and
unquestionably can't fly.*

Given that there's a black Pegasus with an emerald horn standing in the misty path before me, I figure it's completely normal
to freak out. But that's not what has my pulse racing. The
thing is, Pegasus is in the fairy tale I wrote for the contest.
And he looks just like the one standing before me.

I think back to my mom's words about Grandma's pen. Is
this what she was trying to tell me? That the pen brought
stories to life?

If that's the case, then this isn't a dream. It's reality.

And that's when I decide to *really* freak out.

I back away, my traitorous knees buckling under my
weight. My mind races as I try to remember everything I can
about flying horses and if they are dangerous or not.

"Hello," I say, my voice shaking as I crawl backward. I've
no idea if Pegasus even talks, but it's worth a try.

The winged horse steps closer and dips his head as if greet-
ing me. My back bumps into an oak, and I blink a couple of
times just to make sure I'm not hallucinating. The bark cuts
into my back as I sag against it, reminding me that this is real.
This isn't some dream.

A thick mist shrouds the path, obscuring anything beyond
ten feet from me. My own horse has vanished and somehow I

must have reentered this other realm where my fairy tale is unfolding.

Before, when I'd been with the princess, it was fun. But now I'm not so sure. My fairy tale hadn't been all parties, cakes, and sparkling gowns. There had been other things, darker things written on those pages.

The howl of an animal echoes through the forest, sending a spike of terror through me. Using the tree for support, I stand, my legs wobbling, still unsteady from the fall.

The horse treads up to me, so closely his breath blows a stream of hot air against my cheek. Then he nuzzles his nose against my arm as if trying to tell me something. I could lose myself in his eyes, which are the richest black, swirling in endless pools.

The howl rings through the forest again; this time the sound hovers at the edge of the mist. Too close. Feet pound against the mud-packed path, vibrating through the forest. And then through the fog, a pair of green eyes blinks at me. I grab hold of Pegasus, as if he could protect me.

Because even before I can see what's coming, I know what hunts me. This very moment was in my story.

The evil stepsister was known to send her pet wolves to hunt down those who would intrude on her kingdom.

Sure enough. A form races out of the mist. It's a giant black wolf, snarling, with drool dripping off its sharp teeth.

Why oh why did I write that fairy tale? Pegasus nudges me out of panic mode and dips his body down as if telling me to crawl up on his back. The horse is here to save me.

I swing onto Pegasus just as the wolf dives through the air, paws outstretched. The horse takes off, galloping away from the wolf at full speed. I clutch his mane, desperate to stay on.

The horse beats his wings and we rise into the air, flying down the path, cutting through the mist like an arrow released. My heart slams into my chest as we lift higher into the moist air. I can't wrap my mind around what's happening, but as the ground slips farther away, I press myself closer to Pegasus, resting my cheek against his hair.

Seeing the ground so far makes my stomach turn. And yet, it's the most invigorating sensation I could ever imagine. The wind rushes over me, sending my heart tumbling and rolling. The world has become so small and so large all at once.

I've no idea where we are going, but it appears we're veering back around toward the castle. Sure enough, the mist thins like ribbons of silk, revealing the castle rising up from its shrouds.

As we soar closer, shadows cloak the walls, and the spires point upward like knives slashing at the sky. An inky darkness spills from every window except one. A golden gleam streams out of the lone window at the castle's right turret.

Pegasus pumps his wings, drawing us closer to the one golden-lit peak. We edge so close that I can almost touch the castle's turret. I crane my neck to see what is making that golden glow inside.

I nearly cry out in shock.

It's me inside, sitting at a desk that hovers midair in a cobweb-ridden attic. A book rests in my lap, and I'm writing in it with a silvery pen.

The very same pen I took from Dad's drawer. The one I wrote the fairy tale with.

As I write, golden dust curls into the air, swirling above my head like sparkling magic. It drifts across the room and out the window.

Before I have the chance to investigate further, Pegasus swerves around, preparing to land.

"What was that?" I ask the horse. But he doesn't respond, instead beating his wings as he lowers us and lands.

He halts directly in front of the castle's front door and kneels on the bridge as if signaling me to get off. After I dismount, Pegasus neighs, rearing up on his hind legs. I spin around to see what spooked the winged horse and then stumble back in shock. A full pack of wolves is sprinting across the gardens, eyes intent on me.

The horse nudges my back, pushing me toward the front doors, and then turns and gallops away, heading directly toward the wolves.

"No!" I scream at Pegasus.

But it's no use. The horse doesn't turn around. There's only one thing to do. Go through the door. I don't know why Pegasus wanted me to come here, but I know it has to be about what I saw in the window.

The attic and the pen. I must find a way there!

I race to the double doors and throw one open. The butler is nowhere to be found. In fact, the castle appears to be abandoned. The paintings have been slashed, shattered glass litters the ground, and darkness drapes the hallway. Only the trickle of sunbeams seeping in from the windows gives any light.

The howl and snarl of the wolves startles me from my thoughts. I run to the drawing room window to see Pegasus rearing his legs and trampling one of the wolves. But it isn't enough. Two wolves have escaped the horse's onslaught and are heading directly for the castle.

I bolt for the stairs, bounding up them two at a time. Sweat trickles down the sides of my face. My hair clings to my cheeks, and my breath comes out in heavy gasps. When I hit the third floor, I pause, studying the doors.

I've no idea how to reach the attic, I realize.

One by one, I grasp door handle after door handle, but they're all locked. Finally, I come to the last door in the hall. With both hands I seize it. Twisting. Yanking. Crying.

No! I can't die here. In my own fairy tale!

A growl behind me erupts from the silence. Slowly, I peer over my shoulder. It's the wolf from the forest. It's standing directly in front of the stairway, blocking my one escape. Its eyes blaze. It licks its lips hungrily.

Fear claws at my throat, so it's almost impossible to breathe.

"This wasn't the way it was supposed to happen," I say. "This part isn't in my fairy tale."

"No," the wolf says. It talks! How is this happening? "But the moment you entered your fairy tale, you began changing it. And so I have been sent to stop you."

"Stop me?"

"The Word Weavers are not supposed to enter their tales," the wolf says. "You, as a Word Weaver, should know this."

Word Weaver? What is it talking about? I press my back against the locked door, my mind frantically trying to process everything.

"This is just a dream," I say, even though I don't believe it. "I'm going to wake up and all of this will go away."

The wolf chuckles as if I'm an idiot. I know it has every reason to believe that. Because deep down I know this is most definitely not a dream. This is all real and I'm about to be eaten by a wolf.

Who knew that I have so much in common with Red Riding Hood?

The mirror across the hall shimmers, catching my eye. It is full length, edged with gold flowers and vines. The strangest part is that it shows my reflection hovering over nothing but blackness. The door behind me and the floor beneath me have vanished in the mirror, leaving me alone in a void. Then a sizzle of light skitters across the mirror's surface, and my image is replaced by a round face with wide blue eyes and thick red lips.

"What is it you wish for, Word Weaver?" the face within the mirror says, and a hint of a smile pulls on those lips.

This isn't happening. A talking mirror?

"Mirror, mirror on the wall," I whisper, completely desperate to try anything. "Take me back to where I belong."

The light sizzles again, and the round face disappears, revealing a foggy path. The mist parts, showing Bella and Chet riding their horses, calling out my name.

The wolf whips its head, growling in anger. Then it bounds down the hallway toward me. I have about two seconds to save myself.

I don't hesitate. I leap across the hall toward the mirror. I push my arms straight forward so that my body flies parallel to the ground. I'm either going to crack my head open or fly through the mirror to my friends.

Claws scrape across my leg.

But the mirror sucks me inside, wrapping me in mist and magic.

19

Experimental Medical Practices: The best form of getting rid of delusions is to get knocked on the side of the head. If that doesn't work, then we at Experimental Medical Practices believe the situation must be hopeless.

The pounding of horses' hooves wakes me up. I blink against the harsh light as Chet leans down at my side.

"Keira!" Bella splashes through the mud toward me and then wraps me in her arms. "Oh, wow! Are you hurt?"

"No." I moan. "I just got the wind knocked out of me."

"You've got a bad scratch on your leg and it's bleeding," Chet says. *I bet it is,* I think. That horrible wolf raked its claws through me. "Can you stand? Any broken bones?"

Sludgy water drips down my face, but I don't care. I'm so happy to be alive. I wobble on my feet, while Chet and Bella support my arms. "I flew on Pegasus and entered a magical mirror to escape wolves that were trying to kill me. That's where I got the scrap from."

"Uh-oh." Bella scrunches up her face like she's worried for my sanity. "She really did hit her head."

But not Chet. He whistles softly. "You flew on Pegasus? I'm so jealous."

"I need to get back to the castle ASAP," I say. "There's something I need to see."

* * *

Back at the castle, Cheryl applies antiseptic and Band-Aids to my scrape. My fingers jiggle as each second feels like eternity. The moment she's finished, I bolt down the hall and bound up the stairs to our room, ignoring the pain from the scratch on my leg. I throw open my suitcase and toss my clothes onto the floor until I find it.

The pen.

It shimmers in my hand, and a spark of electricity skitters across my skin. I suppose deep down I had known the truth of the pen, but I hadn't wanted to admit it. It's more than a good luck pen. It's a magical pen.

Bella and Chet stumble into the room, panting slightly. They stare at me like I've lost it. I can't imagine how I must look to them. Mud-strewn, wild hair from riding Pegasus, bandaged. Clothes are scattered about the floor, and I'm there sitting in the center of it all.

"Close the door," I say.

Bella hesitates, but Chet quickly follows orders.

"You need to promise to never tell anyone about this." My voice shakes. Maybe it's because I know that, once I voice the pen's true nature, it will make everything more real. "Chet, even your dad. Okay?"

"I'm most definitely in." Chet bounces on his toes like he's ready to climb the canopy bed.

I hold the pen up. Its silvery sheen glistens in the sunlight.

"A pen? That's what this is all about?" Bella sighs, relief flooding her features. "For a second, I thought you were going to tell us something terrible happened."

The lump in my throat grows. "Something terrible has happened. This pen isn't just an ordinary pen. It's magical."

"Magical?" Chet plops down to sit in front of me, scrutinizing the pen. "How does it work? Is it like a genie lamp that grants wishes or turns pumpkins into coaches?"

"Not quite. I think it brings the stories I write to life. Because the fairy tale I wrote seems to be coming alive for me."

"Sweet! Can I try it out?" Chet reaches for the pen, but I snatch it away, tucking it against my muddy shirt.

I don't want to lend him the pen, but then, maybe this would be a good test to see if it does have magical powers. So with shaky fingers, I hand over the journal and pen. Testing my theory may actually be the best first step.

"Now write something," I say. "See if it comes true."

"I'm going to write about how I'm the first eleven-year-old to climb Everest," Chet says. Then he presses the pen's tip to the page and starts writing. I hold my breath.

But nothing happens.

"Hey." Chet holds the pen in the air, scrutinizing it. "This thing doesn't work. I think it needs more ink."

"It hasn't been working for me either, lately. I don't know why." I grab the pen from him and scribble in the corner. Glittery blue ink pours from the tip, spilling onto the paper. Sparkles spin into the air, curling around us as if it's teasing us.

"Sugar and spice." Bella gasps. "What was that? How did you do that sparkly thing?"

"It's the pen," I say in a whisper. "I'm telling you. It's got magical powers. When I write something, it comes true. But ever since I wrote the fairy tale, I keep trying to write, yet it's like I've got writer's block. I don't know what to write. Here, let me try to write something."

The pen bursts to life and ink begins to flow.

A magical rope swings from the top turret of the castle.

But I don't write any further, because Chet exclaims, "Hot fire! This is wild stuff." Chet's on his feet again, pacing back and forth before me. "I've got an idea for a story! Write about the three of us as pirates. I want to have a ship all to myself and a shiny sword with a hilt packed full of gems."

"Pirates?"

"Definitely not pirates." Bella scrunches up her face like she's tasted sour candy. "Write a story about me becoming a famous designer!"

"And make it a fun story," Chet continues. He picks up the fire poker and slashes the air with it. Then he jumps up on the bed, swinging around the bedpost, brandishing the poker like he's fighting off a horde of scoundrels.

Hearing them speak, my fingers twitch and the pen warms in my hand. The aching need to write with the pen overwhelms me, but suddenly fear mingles with that desperation. What if I write about a horrible monster like that wolf? What if something goes wrong and a murdering stepsister forms out of the words I create? "Guys," I say weakly. "Please stop. I don't think I should write any more stories."

"I can't decide where I want my designs to appear in," Bella says, completely ignoring my worries.

"Or maybe I should climb K2 because technically that's the harder peak to climb."

My hand shakes and sweat pours down my face. Bella's and Chet's voices fade away. The pen is sapphire. It's an ocean, full of frothing waves and the deepest indigo depths. Its cerulean skies stretch beyond into an unknown land of mystery and intrigue.

A wind cuts across my face, slashing my hair against my cheeks and spraying sea salt on my lips. I taste the salt, and the sound of steel clashing against steel vibrates through my being. My balance is off, so I steady myself on the shifting boat.

There's a sword in my hand and before me is Chet, grinning that devilish grin of his. A sea serpent rises up from the depths. Its emerald scales glint in the sun's rays and its giant eye blinks at us as if we'd be a lovely lunch.

A scream escapes from me. But apparently, Chet isn't daunted. Unlike me, he lets out a loud whoop, darting his sword into the air.

I see it all. I feel it. I'm living it.

So I write like one possessed. The words spill out of my pen and I can't form my letters fast enough. I'm caught in a maelstrom of words, spinning and churning, and it's wildly intoxicating.

Until hands grab me. Someone rips the pen from my hand. The magic's presence scatters and my heart dives into utter despair.

20

Sleuthing 101: Any good spy can beat a lie detector test. You just have to convince yourself you're right!

"Give it back!" I scream, clawing at the air. "I need it. The story isn't finished!"

And then the world shifts. I'm no longer gazing out on endless sea or monsters. Chet and Bella are hunkered before me, worried expressions on their faces.

I hold up my hand. "Where's my sword?" I whisper.

"Did you write it?" Chet's eyes are ablaze, full of fire and thrill.

"Keira!" Bella shakes me. "You've got to pull yourself together. Your mom is coming!"

"Keira! Bella!" It's Mom calling to us from down the hall.

"Oh no." What have I done? I'm so dazed after being ripped out of my writing world that it's hard to orient myself.

Bella kicks my journal under the bed and tucks the pen in the folds of the bedspread just as Mom steps into the room.

"Hey, girls," she says. "Oh, and hello, Chet. How was horseback riding?"

"Great." I plaster on a fake smile. "How was your museum trip? Did you learn lots of new facts about France?"

But Mom isn't fooled. Her brow furrows, first over the

clothes scattered about, and then her eyes widen as she takes in my muddy clothes. "Are you bleeding? What happened?"

"I'm fine," I lie. Bella's eyebrows rise in a *yeah, right* expression while Chet coughs, staring at the golden tapestry. "Okay, so maybe I'm not. I fell off the horse, landed in a mud puddle, and hit my head."

"She thinks she flew on Pegasus," Bella adds. "And was chased by wolves. She's not feeling so well, Mrs. Harding."

I flash a glare at Bella.

"Pegasus? Wolves?" Mom draws closer, her frown deepening by the second. Her eyes flick to the lump in the bedspread. "Are you hiding something, girls?"

Neither of us says a word, but my heart is pounding so loud I'm sure everyone can hear it.

"Let me see it."

I hold my breath as I withdraw the pen. The heat has vanished along with the glow of the magic, but just as before, the desperation to clutch it tightly against my chest pulls at me. The pen sparkles as if it is saying hello to my mom.

Mom's eyes grow wide and she gasps. I cringe, waiting for her wrath. But at the same time, there's a sense of relief that I don't need to lie to her anymore.

"It's the pen from Dad's dresser," I lament. "You were right. I wrote the fairy tale for the contest with it."

"Oh, Keira." Mom's whole body trembles as she staggers to sit on the bed. "Put that thing away! You must get it out of my sight."

"What's so bad about a pen?" Bella asks as I tuck the pen back into the zipper pouch of my suitcase.

"Can I try writing with it again?" Chet says. "Maybe this time it will work for me."

"No!" Mom jerks to standing, holding out both hands as if to stop a storm. "Bella, Chet. You need to leave now. And close the door behind you."

After the door closes, Mom makes a tent with her hands, pressing her fingertips to her lips. "Maybe I'm overreacting," she mutters to herself. "It's just a fairy tale, right?"

"Mom"—I brace myself for the horrible truth I know is coming—"does this pen have powers?"

"Yes, it does." Mom releases a long, agonized breath. "Great powers. But only if it's used by a Word Weaver."

I gasp. "That's what the wolf called me."

"Wolf?"

"Yes, it's complicated. But I think I entered my fairy tale. And there's a wolf in my fairy tale. He said something about me being a Word Weaver."

"You talked with a character from your story?" Mom shoots up from the bed a second time and clenches my shoulders.

"Yeah, is that bad?"

"Yes, very. It's completely against the rules of the Word Weavers. Once we write a story, we are not allowed to enter the tale or alter it. If we do, the story will retaliate and has the right to exterminate us or lock us within that story as captives forever."

"Us?"

"Yes. Us." She draws me into a fierce hug, her body trembling. "I didn't want to ever bring you into this. Your grandma felt the tradition should be carried on. That's why she sent the pen to me. But I disagreed with her. Being Word Weavers, we are given a huge responsibility, too huge, if you ask me." Mom releases me, sagging now onto the bed and hanging her head. "So I hid the pen and made a vow to never write another story again. It's been nearly impossible to resist the temptation to write. That's why I had to make all of those rules, get rid of the writing utensils, throw out books. It has been so hard. So very hard."

"I don't understand. What's a Word Weaver?"

"Someone who can write with that pen and the story will come to life. No one else has that ability. We also have the extreme need to write stories. It's basically torture for us to not write."

It all makes sense. Why I have always been secretly obsessed with writing. And why Mom has been so against it. "Is that why you're always writing lists and facts?"

"Yes." Mom gives a hopeless laugh. "The need to write is so powerful. You are just now getting a glimpse of the compulsion to write that you must bear. But after making the horrible mistake of using the pen and writing my own story, I told myself I'd never write another story. Even if it wasn't with the pen. I deal with the obsession by only writing facts."

"Why didn't you just tell me?"

"There are powerful people who wish to control Word Weavers for themselves," Mom says. "Remember those men who broke into our house. They were after the pen. And maybe one of us. So I knew I needed to protect you. If someone were to ever come and ask you about it, you would know nothing. I have worked so hard to keep our secret. I have to admit that I hoped the Word Weaver gene had skipped you, or if you didn't know about it, it wouldn't control you as strongly as it had me."

I cross my arms, looking out the window. "You said Grandma sent you the pen. She didn't feel that way, did she?"

"No, which is why your grandma isn't alive anymore." Mom's eyes harden and she gulps in a shuddered breath.

"They killed her?"

"Yes. No." Mom shakes her head and begins picking up all the clothes from the floor and folding them into neat stacks. Tears stream from her eyes. "Honestly, I don't know what to believe anymore. The important thing is to not panic." Mom puts a stack of clothes in the suitcase. "We must stay focused on the facts and go from there."

"Okay," I say weakly.

And in that moment, everything clarifies for me. Just like Mom, I suddenly need facts. Because without them, my world has tilted just enough so that nothing looks quite the same anymore. She needed the facts for their solidity, their grounding.

"Tell me exactly what you wrote. Maybe we can figure out a way to fix this."

So I retell my whole fairy tale of the princess and stepsister.

"It began when the stepsister got jealous at her sister's birthday party. The princess fell in love with the same prince as the stepsister fell in love with." I finger the edge of my riding habit as I realize I'd experienced that moment of the story only the other day.

"Then people at the castle start disappearing," I continue. "The stepsister was taking them into her tower, one by one, each Friday night at the stroke of midnight."

"What happens at the end?" Mom asks.

"At the ball, the stepsister reveals herself as the one who has been kidnapping all of the servants of the castle. The stepsister tells the princess she did it so she could have the prince for herself. Then the princess would be alone forever."

"What a horrible story!"

"I know." I hang my head. "I got mad at you, and I don't know why I wrote it. It was supposed to be a ghost story with a twist."

"Some twist," Mom huffs as she snaps the suitcase closed. "So this is what we are going to do. We're going to leave here as soon as I can get a cab and a flight out of Paris."

"We're leaving? Do we have to? It's not like this story can hurt us, right?"

"There are a lot of things at stake here, Keira. First, the fairy tale has already come to life. It will play out whether you want it to or not. Second, if we aren't careful, we may get the attention of the same people who broke into our house. They want the pen. And your story may gain too much attention, if it hasn't already."

"But isn't there something I can do? Like use the pen to rewrite the end or change the story? The princess says she needs my help. And what if that maid from last week didn't quit but was really taken by the stepsister? I can't live with the idea that I caused people to disappear, and especially not be trapped in that fairy tale realm!"

"I know it's hard to deal with this, but it isn't that simple." Mom smooths down my hair and kisses my forehead. "I wish I knew how to fix things. Now, I'm going to make some calls. You stay here and don't get yourself into trouble. Oh, and take this." Mom hands me a laminated card. It reads: *Ways to Deal with Stressful Situations*.

"It always makes me feel better in times of distress," Mom says. "Sometimes I just write the list over and over if the need to write with the pen becomes too great."

Then she kisses me again and leaves.

I'm a Word Weaver. I bring stories to life, terrifying and magical ones. The power of who I am and what I can do is more than any twelve-year-old should have.

Fact: A portrait is an artwork that has been created to represent a person. Mind you, it is not the actual person or an apparition of that person.

Thursday (Jeudi), June 17th

Last night I hardly slept. My dreams were filled with ghosts and flying horses and snarling wolves.

So when the door bursts open this morning, banging hard against the wall, I pick up both pillows, jump out of bed, and fling them at the intruders. But it's only Bella and Chet standing in the doorway. Bella's biting her nails, while Chet's hair sticks up like a porcupine's.

"Hey!" Bella holds up her hands. "It's just us. Your friends."

"Sorry," I mumble, and then peek inside my suitcase to make sure my pen is still tucked. After Mom told me all that stuff about how those burglars were actually after the pen, I'm starting to think I need a better hiding place for it.

"While you were sleeping the day away, Chet and I were wandering the castle." Bella wrings her hands. "And, well. Maybe I'm starting to think you're not so crazy after all. I found her."

"Who?"

"Your ghost!" Bella cries. "Follow me."

The three of us dash down the corridor to the back of the castle. Bella and Chet race into the ballroom, but I falter at the landing. The ballroom, usually bright and cheerful with its walls lined with windows tucked inside arched alcoves, is cloaked in dark shadows that stretch across the cold marble floor.

Outside, the wind gusts and sings a chilling tune. The long rectangular room lies barren except for an occasional cushioned bench stationed along the cream-colored walls. A heaviness pulls at me.

"Keira!" Bella shouts from midway down the hall. "Come on!"

I need to stop acting like such a wimp. So I toss my hair over my shoulder, lift my chin, and march down the ballroom steps and over to where Chet and Bella stand under a painting, staring. It's the same painting whose eyes moved on my first day here at Chenonceau.

"It's the princess," I whisper. "The one I keep seeing as a ghost in my fairy-tale realm."

"Fairy-tale realm or not," Chet says, "this chick was a real person. Her name was Gabrielle d'Estrées."

Chet points to the gold plate under the princess's portrait. It reads: *Gabrielle d'Estrées, 1573–1599.*

"So now we know she really is real." I gaze at the princess's eyes, expecting them to move and stare back. But they stay true to their oils, unseeing.

"There's more. Just wait a second," Bella says, her voice hushed. "She might do it again. Last time we were here, her mouth moved and she said something. I'm going to have nightmares until the day I die."

"She was speaking in French," Chet says. "I think she said, 'Help me.'"

"She wants us to help her, I know." How do I explain to a portrait that there isn't any way to change my story? Even Mom said it wasn't possible. "I wish there was something we could do, but it isn't like the ghost is actually real or things can be changed. What happened, happened."

"Maybe." Bella chews her bottom lip. "It's just so tragic. We need to do something to help her!"

"Speaking of tragedy," I say, grimacing, "my mom thinks we need to leave."

"What?! But we can't leave. It will ruin everything! The ball is tomorrow. All my design work is arriving, and I have to be here when it's being showcased."

"Bummer." Chet scuffs his sneaker over the marble floor. "This was amping up to be a fun summer holiday after all."

"But this ghost was once a real person, right?" Bella reminds me. "She needs our help."

I suck in a deep breath. Bella is right. I can't just abandon Gabrielle. She's depending on me. "It's time to do some research. We need to find out more about this Gabrielle and what really happened to her. Maybe we can find some answers in the library."

"There you are!" Ms. Teppernat shrieks from the steps and then clamors down in her black high-heel boots. "We've been looking everywhere for you, and here you are! All ready to learn!"

Cheryl scampers up behind Ms. Teppernat, followed by Chet's dad and a lady wearing a black leotard and a black dance skirt with her brown hair twisted into a bun. She has a sharp fox-like nose and thin lips pressed together.

"Learn?" I'm so confused that I don't even know how to escape the Dragon.

"The dances you'll have to perform for the ball on Friday," Ms. Teppernat says. She waves her hands so furiously that the bangles trailing up her arms clang like bells.

"Er—" Chet stammers. "I'm late for—you know. So I'll be seeing you guys around."

"Oh, but we were hoping you would help the girls out." Cheryl dives sideways to block Chet's path. "This way they will have someone else to dance with at the ball. And you'll help give them a little practice."

"Not so fast, son," Mr. Parker says, lifting his eyebrows meaningfully at Chet. "I think this will be a great opportunity for you."

Chet scowls, but when his dad clears his throat and crosses his arms, Chet says, "I guess I could carve out a few minutes. But it will cost you."

"Fine," Ms. Teppernat says. "Since you already signed the waiver for the horseback riding, Cheryl will add this position. But for this event, we will need to make up a contract. He must follow the expected times and obligations, such as arrive at the ball on time and dance with each girl for exactly five minutes."

"I'm sure Chet can handle that," Mr. Parker says.

"Two minutes." Chet gulps. "That's my final offer."

While Ms. Teppernat, Cheryl, and Mr. Parker continue ironing out the logistics with Chet, Bella points to Ms. Teppernat's back and sticks her fingers on top of her head like horns. It takes everything in me to suppress my giggles, but then I freeze when Ms. Teppernat spins to face me.

Cringing, I half expect the Dragon to breathe fire, but Ms. Teppernat surprises me by grabbing my shoulders and staring me down.

"Whatever happens on Friday night," she says, "the most important thing is to smile and pretend everything is perfect. Do you understand?"

"Why do I have to pretend everything is perfect?"

"What if the ghost shows up?" Chet asks.

"Ignore it." Ms. Teppernat pats my cheeks as if ghosts showing up is completely normal. "If you ignore the ghost, it will ignore you. Are we clear on how this is going to play out?"

Chet's mouth hangs open. "You believe in the ghost, too?"

"You think the ghost is coming to the ball?" Bella starts back up with her nail biting. If things continue to get worse, she's not going to have any more nails to bite.

"Ugh." Ms. Teppernat presses her fingers against the temples of her forehead. "All these questions are such an annoyance. Can we focus on the task at hand?"

"Yes, of course!" Cheryl nods vigorously. "Please let me introduce you to your dance instructor, Madame Simone."

The black-leotard lady glides over to us. She tilts her head to the side and dips into an elegant curtsy.

"*Bonjour,*" she says in a lilting French accent. "Today you shall learn the waltz. We shall begin with Debussy's 'Clair de lune.'"

Gracefully, she sets her music player on one of the benches and with her long finger pushes PLAY. The chords of the piano fill the room with its aching and haunting tune.

Then she draws Chet and me to face each other, saying, "Hold hands like this."

She puts my left hand in Chet's right, and then places my right hand on his shoulder.

Chet jumps back. "Whoa. No one said I had to hold her hand."

Mr. Parker reminds Chet of his agreement, which personally I think is a little odd that his dad would be so adamant that he dance with me. Chet huffs and rolls his eyes, but ends up getting back into position. Mr. Parker nods before leaving.

Normally, I would've laughed over Chet's squeamishness, but I can't shake the feeling that something is off. A shiver of wind rushes through the room as the instructor barks out "one, two, three, four" over the music. Satisfied that Madame Simone has everything under control, Ms. Teppernat and Cheryl leave the ballroom to meet with the caterer.

Then the large grandfather clock in the main entry begins to chime. My muscles tense, and I'm hoping, begging for it to stop at nine, but nope. It keeps chiming until it reaches twelve strokes. Something nags me about the clock. Why does it ring twelve strokes at random times and never at midnight?

I'm also finding it hard to concentrate when Madame Simone yells out numbers and cuts her hand through the air like a knife.

"Man," Chet whispers. "She sure takes her job seriously."

"Box step!" Madame Simone shouts. "Box step!"

"This lady missed her calling," Chet says as we shuffle about. "She should've signed up for the military."

"Um—" I begin.

The center of the ballroom shimmers like a heat wave over a lake. One by one, the flickering waves morph into forms. People! Soon ghosts pack the entire ballroom, swirling about in voluminous ball gowns and glittering gems.

"Non!" Madame Simone frowns at Chet and me, jerking my mind back to our little dance group. *"This* is not the box step. *This* is not dancing."

"You're right." Chet lets go of me and crosses his arms. *"This* is so stupid. I don't know what a box step is."

"You must make box with your feet," Madame Simone says. She backs up and nearly bumps into two ghosts drinking from fluted glasses, laughing soundlessly. "Like so."

"How can you possibly focus when *they* are in the room?" I say.

"Who's in the room?" Bella says.

"The ghosts!"

This causes Madame Simone, Bella, and Chet to turn around and face the center of the ballroom.

Madame Simone gasps.

Bella shrieks.

And Chet says, "Jumping crickets! It's a room full of ghosts!"

Madame Simone begins screaming hysterically and rattles off something in French as she races to collect her music player. The cord rips out of the wall as Madame Simone dashes out of the ballroom, still screaming.

The moment she unplugs the music, the ghosts vanish.

"What happened?" Bella says, clutching me. "Where did all of those ghosts go?"

"I honestly don't know," I say with a nervous laugh. "But look at the bright side—now we don't have to have dancing class."

Chet grins. "I'm beginning to like these ghosts."

"Come on," I say. "We need to go to the library and get some answers before anyone finds us and puts us to work."

* * *

"Nothing here about a ghost," Chet says, after reading through the section on Gabrielle d'Estrées in the *Historical Annals of Chenonceau*.

The three of us huddle around the table in the library, where Chet has the book laid out for us to see.

"That's good, though," I say. "It means the fairy tale I wrote isn't actually real. It's just a fairy tale."

"Wait." Chet's eyes grow larger as he reads on. "There's more. It's just hard to translate."

Then he takes a piece of paper and writes down some notes. Finally, he looks up and says, "So from what I can tell, over four hundred years ago, there was a duchess named Gabrielle d'Estrées."

"The girl in the painting!" Bella says.

"Yeah. And she was in love with a prince who became the king of France. His name was"—Chet checks his notes—"Henry IV. There was a problem. The duchess had a stepsister. And she hated Gabrielle. Well, this is more like speculation than history."

"Oh, I love gossip!" Bella perches on the edge of her chair.

"There's a stepsister in this story?" A hollow emptiness guts my stomach.

"Yep. But no one realized how jealous her stepsister was. Not even Gabrielle." Chet holds his hands up like he's really getting into the story. "Now, Gabrielle told her stepsister her deepest secret. The king had offered his hand in marriage."

Bella sighs. "How romantic."

"They decided to announce their engagement at a huge party to celebrate."

"Was it here?" I ask, not really wanting the answer.

Chet scans through the *Annals* and nods.

"By 'party,' do you mean a ball?" Bella says.

"Right," Chet says. "Ball. So the *ball* was here at Chenonceau where Henry and Gabrielle planned to announce their engagement to all of France."

"Why do I have a feeling something went wrong," Bella says.

"Yep, you're right. Before the ball finished—"

"The duchess died," I interrupt. "The stepsister convinced the king to marry another, specifically herself. But the king, heartbroken, married someone else who he really didn't love."

Chet studies me and then his notes. "Um, yeah. It was Marie de Médicis that he married. Not a happy marriage. And he did wear black after Gabrielle died. He was the first monarch to do that."

"So no one was happy and therefore there was no happily ever after," I finish in a breathless whisper.

Bella gawks at me. "This is exactly how your story goes, isn't it?"

"Yep." I shuffle to the window and gaze into the lingering mist. My stomach won't stop churning. "We have to do something, guys. I can't just stand here knowing I was the cause of so many people's unhappiness."

"Maybe this isn't your fault," Bella says. "What if you heard this story somewhere and you unintentionally wrote it. Like it was in your subconscious."

"No. This royal mess of a story is mine and it's all my fault. Somehow I'm going to fix it. I have to make things right."

"So basically you think that Gabrielle d'Estrées was murdered? Maybe even by Marie de Médicis?" Chet says. "And their ghosts still haunt this castle today?"

"That pretty much sums it up." Shaking my head, I sag into one of the wingback chairs.

"Hey, something else is interesting here." Chet pulls out another book and starts thumbing through it. "This is the history of everyone who ever owned this castle."

"My mom would love that book," I say.

"According to this book, Monsieur Monteque has only owned this place for about four months."

"That's not long ago," I say. "It was after I won the contest."

We talk some more, but come up with no solutions. I sag against the back of my chair.

"If we can fix all of this," Bella says, "do you think your mom will let us stay for the ball?"

"I don't know if I can leave until I fix this mess. I can't live with myself knowing I was the cause and still am the cause of people disappearing. Maybe even being murdered."

"There's gotta be a way to solve this," Chet says.

"Maybe." I sit straighter, a new idea forming in my mind. "There's something we need to check out. Something Pegasus showed me."

*Decision–Making Advice: If you think it's a bad idea,
then most likely it is.*

"Are you sure this is a good idea?" Bella won't stop biting her nails.

"No," I say. "But I don't have a better one, either."

The three of us stare at the attic door, hesitating. This was the door I tried to open when the wolf cornered me in my fairy tale. Either it's just a typical attic or it conceals a magical book like the one I saw when I flew on Pegasus.

"Madame did say it was off-limits." Chet hands me the key. "So my vote is to definitely check it out."

"I don't know, guys," Bella says. "What if the Wicked Witch of the West catches us?"

"It's going to be completely safe," I say, trying to calm her. "But how about this. You stay here and watch the door. If anyone tries to come up, flick the light twice."

I slide the key into the keyhole. It fits perfectly. The lock snaps, and with little resistance, I'm able to turn the knob. The door creaks as it opens, letting out a burst of stale air. The three of us peer up into the darkness. A small hallway covered in a thick layer of dust leads to a stairwell.

My pulse quickens as I step inside and trail my hand across the wall, searching for a light switch. My hand slides over one and I switch it on. Two sconce lights flicker to life, their bulbs dusty and yellowed, reminding me of jack-o'-lanterns.

"Good luck!" Bella squeaks as we head up the stairs. "Please don't die."

"If the Wicked Witch walks by," Chet warns, "just close the door. We don't want her finding out that we're up here."

This stairwell is identical to the two others below with two flights and a landing between them. Except this stairwell is wooden, unlike the others lined with carpet. The papered walls are deteriorated and holes are scratched into them, probably by mice.

As I climb the stairs, I paw the air in front of me to make sure my path is cobweb-free. Strips of fallen wallpaper are in heaps on the stairs, and dust billows around me. At the landing's crest, I hesitate. Would the ghost be standing there when I turn the corner? Goose bumps course up my arms.

"You all right?" Chet asks.

"Yeah. Fine." But my quivering voice betrays me.

I round the corner to find the upper flight of stairs, lit by a third sconce. No ghost here; only a large cobweb blocks my path.

At the top is an entrance into another hall, this one smaller than the ones below. A large window faces out the front of the castle, allowing only a weak wedge of light inside due to dust and grime. Two doors open up into rooms on either side of the hall. I take the first one, while Chet checks out the other. The room is empty except for a fireplace and window. I move to the corner where the light had shown out of the turret that should've been attached to this room, but it's just a wall.

I sigh. There is no secret room. No book. No glittery golden light. Maybe I imagined the whole thing. But more likely, the room exists only in my fairy-tale realm. I rub my head. Everything is so confusing.

"Keira!" Chet calls from the other room. "Come here!"

Running, I cross the hall to join Chet. He holds up a pair of shoes for me.

"I found my climbing shoes."

"That's so weird! Why would they be up here?"

"They weren't the only thing I found." He swoops his hand. "Look around you."

The room mirrors the room I just checked out. Except that here all kinds of junk are strewn across the floor, perched on the fireplace mantel, and hanging over a lone chair parked in the center of the room.

"But why?" I walk to the mantel and eye the clutter on it. "Wait a sec. Look, binoculars! These look exactly like Ms. Jones's." Then I pick up a sparkly bracelet. "My mom's bracelet!"

"Does this look familiar?" Chet sticks a set of earbuds into his ears.

"That's my music player, isn't it? Give that to me, silly!"

He wags his head side to side as he listens to music. I snatch it out of his hands.

"Why is all this stuff up here? Chet, are you even listening? All this belongs to us. The people staying here. It's been stolen."

Chet knits his brows, finally seeming to take the situation more seriously. "I think it was the ghost."

"Really?" I roll my eyes. "Ghosts can't carry things."

"Anything is possible." He shrugs. "But I think it's time to go to the police with this information. Hey, it's more than a figure floating through the halls. It's a thief!"

"No one's going to believe us." I rummage through a pile of clothes on the floor. I dig up a pair of my shorts and Bella's purple dress. "I mean really, what do we say? 'Mr. Policeman, a ghost took random stuff of ours and put it in the attic.' Hello! We'd be like the laughingstock of the French police. What we need is evidence. The real deal."

"Yeah. I guess you're right."

Hugging my newfound possessions, I wander to the front window.

I sigh in frustration as I rub a hole through the grime and gaze below to the castle grounds. The storm has passed, leaving behind puddles, glistening trees leaves, and baby-blue skies. Two figures catch my eye, hurrying down the oak-lined road toward the castle. Mr. Jones is lugging a large package in the shape of a mirror.

"Hey, Chet. It's Mr. and Mrs. Jones. What are they doing now?"

Chet scrubs a hole for himself. "He must be strong to carry that big a package."

"That or younger than we think. But the question is, what's in that package?"

"You really don't trust anybody, do you?"

"I've been training myself to be a detective ever since I snuck a copy of a Nancy Drew book and read it," I say. "It might be proving to be more helpful than I thought it would be."

"We should get back before Madame catches us here."

I take one last look at the thin rectangular package in Mr. Jones's arms. "I'm going to find out what that is."

Back on the second floor, Bella nearly tackles me.

"You're still alive!" Bella says. "I didn't know if you'd survive! Did you find what you were looking for?"

"No, but look, I found a bunch of your stuff that you said had gone missing."

"In the attic? Now, that's weird."

"My thoughts exactly."

*Fact: When conducting a stakeout, observe any and all
suspicious activity. Record your findings, preferably
with photographs or video.*

"If we hurry," Chet says, "we can confront Mr. Jones!"

Bella and I fly down the stairs, trying to keep up with
Chet. But when we reach the first floor, Mr. Jones is nowhere
to be seen.

"Where did he go?" I search the surrounding areas.

"I say we split up," Chet says. "I'll do reconnaissance out
front while, Bella, you take the back, and, Keira, you scout
around the house."

"Since when did we join the military?" Bella crosses her
arms as Chet sprints toward the front doors.

The butler calmly opens a door to let Chet out and then
shuts it again. Not once did his expression change. But just
before he closes the door, I think I glimpse my mom walking
up the lane.

"Mom!" I bolt for the front door, where once again the
butler opens it just at the right moment so I don't even have to
slow down.

Sure enough, it is Mom clipping up the pebbled path. This
morning she's wearing a simple pale green dress, a thin belt
cinched at the waist, and tan Skechers. That is something

about Mom. Her clothes are always practical and simple, but she manages to look pretty in whatever she wears.

Curtains of sunlight filter through the oaks onto the path. The trees appear as if they've been hosed down with emerald dye, they're so rich and bright, and alongside the path, flowers bloom in rainbows of colors.

"Keira!" Mom's voice quivers, breaking the magic of the world around us. Once again I'm reminded that things aren't quite right at Chenonceau. "Is everything okay?"

"I don't know. We found a bunch of the stuff that had gone missing in the attic. And we think Mr. and Mrs. Jones are up to something. They're acting awfully suspicious. Did you get the tickets?"

"Yes." Mom wraps her arm around me. "The soonest flight I could get was tomorrow at noon. I would've liked to leaver earlier, but it will have to do. We'll have to tell Bella. She'll be devastated. But what I'm really concerned about is I think I was followed."

I glance over my shoulder, but nothing moves along the path except some leaves flittering down from the trees.

"You don't look so good, Mom."

"Yes, well, I haven't had a chance to review today's fact." Mom digs through her purse until she finds her fact book. "Here it is: 'Outside North and South America, the only alligators found in the wild are in China.' There. That's rather interesting, don't you think? I feel better already."

"Riiight. No gators here!" But I most decidedly did *not* feel better knowing that there aren't alligators in France. Because there are ghosts and people following us and strange guests at the castle.

"I think I'm going to lie down now," she says as we stride past the butler and into the castle. "I've got a headache coming on."

*   *   *

"Did you find them?" Chet is panting and sweating like a horse.

"Who?"

"The Joneses!"

"Oh! Yes," I say. "They're in their room. I tried listening outside their door, but the Wicked Witch of the West walked by and told me how impossibly rude I was. I'm embarrassed to say I was compromised."

"That's a bummer. Because a stakeout is a really great idea."

"Police do stakeouts. Sleuths infiltrate or complete covert operations." I groan at how I seem to be failing left and right. "I really need to work on my skills."

"Speaking of skills, I'm going to do a little rock climbing." Chet pats a big black bag slung over his shoulder. "Got all my gear now that I've got my shoes back. Want to come?"

"Rock climbing? Where?"

"On the castle."

"Madame will murder you if she catches you."

"Guess I better not get caught, then!"

Fact: In France, it is unacceptable to eat
pommes frites *with your fingers.*

Candlelight flickers on everyone's face as we sit around the dining room table for dinner. Mrs. Jones apologizes for her husband's tardiness.

"He's feeling a little off today," Mrs. Jones says in a shrill voice.

"Would that be because he was carrying such a large package?" I ask nonchalantly as I butter my roll.

Mrs. Jones's fork freezes midway to her mouth. "Why, yes, perhaps it is. Or maybe it's from all of the horrid noises at night and so many things that have gone missing. I am convinced that this castle is haunted!"

Chet spits out his water, while Mom chokes on her steak.

"Perhaps we should call the experts to deal with these thefts," Mrs. Jones says. "I am quite terrified for all of our safety!"

"Then perhaps you should consider leaving?" Madame says.

"I don't think that will be necessary," Mom says hurriedly, patting her chest and clearing her throat. "Just today, Keira and Chet found all of the missing items in the attic. Someone must have been playing a prank on us."

Mom is right. The last thing we need is any media attention

on us or an association with strange events. That would be a great way to alert the men who had been trying to steal the pen to our location.

"They were in the attic?" Madame clucks her tongue. "That is forbidden area."

"We were only trying to find our stuff," I say, omitting the part about the secret room.

Mr. Jones hobbles into the dining room, waving his hands about. "Dreadfully sorry!" he says. "I had a business call and then my leg was acting up a bit and I had a time of it getting down for dinner."

"You are excused," Madame says gravely. "Do sit and join us."

A servant brings an *entrecôte* steak for him and dessert for the rest of us, which Madame calls *profiteroles au chocolat*. I spoon up a mouthful of the ice-cream puff. The hot chocolate sauce mixed with the cold ice cream creates the perfect palette combination. Too bad I'm so upset that I can't totally enjoy it.

"I hope you found deenner *delicieux*?" the cook says in her gravelly voice, seeming to appear out of nowhere. She looms over the group at the far end of the table, holding something behind her back.

"It was divine." Bella claps her hands.

"It was suitable," Madame concedes. "Now, if you'll serve the coffee."

"Bon," the cook continues as if Madame had never spoken. "Zis ees the last meal I cook een *le château*. I am quitting!"

"You cannot do this!" Madame shoots up from her chair, her face as red as a hot pepper. She switches to French, rattling away as fast as her mouth can flap.

My mind spins. The cook can't leave! I haven't had the chance to talk to her again. There's still so much I want to ask her.

"Cook, please," I beg. "You must stay until we leave."

"At least until after the ball," Bella says.

"Mademoiselle," the cook says. "Zis ees why I leave. Too many deesappearances and strange ghosts lurking about. And zis Friday—eet weell not be me!"

"What is she talking about?" Bella says.

Chet's dad chuckles. "She's a crazy loon." He lifts his glass in the air as if for a toast.

"And you." The cook thrusts a gnarly finger at Mr. Parker. "You lie. You are zee famous Canadian actor, Shan Valrose."

From behind her back, she withdraws a tabloid magazine and tosses it onto the table. Then with a smirk on her face, she stalks out of the room.

Everyone leans over the table to peer at the magazine. The page shows the latest celebrity happenings. At the bottom is a photograph of a man stepping out of a limo, waving to the paparazzi. The article beside it is titled: "Shan Valrose: Actor Turned Spy?"

Mrs. Jones clucks her tongue. Mom gasps, her fork clattering onto the table. Quickly, I skim the article. The cook is onto something here. Apparently, Valrose wasn't getting any new movie deals, so he turned to becoming a hired spy for extra income.

"An actor?" Mr. Parker clears his throat and chuckles. "There's a first for everything."

I study Mr. Parker. There's no doubt that the two pictures are similar. Except in the photo, Mr. Parker's hair is bleached blond instead of black, and he doesn't have a mustache. Whether or not Shan Valrose and Chet's dad are one and the same, they sure look oddly similar.

"Oh, so exciting." Bella digs through her purse and withdraws a pen. She turns to Chet's dad. "Can I have your autograph?"

But I snatch the magazine and slap it in front of Chet. "Is it true? Are you really a spy? And if so, who are you working for?"

Chet's face crumples as if he has been told a comet is about to destroy the Earth. Slowly, he slides under the table, disappearing.

But Mr. Parker merely shrugs, saying, "Complimentary of course, but total blasphemy."

I open my mouth to argue, but a nightmarish scream erupts from down the hall.

Fact: The first known waltz was at a peasant dance in Provence, France, in 1559.

Everyone at the table jumps and rushes toward the sound. It came from the ballroom. Turning the corner, Chet nearly runs over Renee, one of the maids, who is screaming. She wears a black dress and white apron. Her eyes are wild and her cap hangs askew on the side of her head. She clings to Chet and rattles off something in French, her breath coming out in heavy gasps.

"She says she saw a ghost," Chet tells the group.

Renee faints and collapses in his arms. I roll my eyes at the maid's dramatics. *Really, she couldn't have been that scared.* But Madame's face hardens. She pushes through the dazed group to march into the ballroom.

Madame cries out. *"Oh là là!"*

The group follows. Every window—over a dozen—has been smashed. The tapestries, shredded, now flutter around the ballroom. If what Renee says is true, then this ghost is capable of destruction. Or threatening the living.

"Good heavens!" Mrs. Jones cries, fanning herself. "Whatever has happened? Is this the workings of the ghost?"

"My beautiful ballroom!" Madame staggers down the steps and across the ballroom floor. The rest of the group hurries after her. My shoes crunch on broken glass. Madame stops at a painting. Its canvas is ragged and torn from what appears to be claw marks.

"This painting doesn't belong here." Piecing it back together, Madame studies it closer. "In fact, the painting that belongs here is missing!"

"What painting is missing, Madame?" I say.

"King Henry IV." Madame sets the painting aside and rubs her forehead. This is the first time I've seen Madame lose her cool. "It must be found. She will be furious to find it missing."

"She?" I say.

"I mean 'he.' Monsieur, of course."

I pick up the painting and patch together its tatters. It's a landscape of hills dotted with flowers. Wait a second. I bet this is what Mr. Jones was carrying today. It isn't a mirror. It's a painting! Swiveling around, I face Mrs. Jones.

"This countryside painting is yours," I say. "You bought it today!"

"What poppycock is this? Of course we bought a painting, but ours is safely tucked away in our room." Mrs. Jones steps closer to the painting I'm holding and inspects it. "My, my. There's quite a resemblance."

"If what you say is true," Madame says, "you won't mind showing us your painting."

"I'll go check," Chet offers.

"Hurry." Madame hands him a key.

"Do you think it was the ghost who did this or a person?" I ask Madame.

"What does it matter?" Madame snaps. "Despite my protests, Monsieur is determined that there is to be a ball tomorrow in this very room and somehow this place must be presentable. Monsieur will not be pleased and if he is not pleased—"

She trails off and I realize the truth. She could lose her job over this. Which means there's no way that she had any part in this destruction.

"Oh, the ball!" Bella cries. "Do you think it will be canceled?"

"Wouldn't that be a shame," Mrs. Jones says, yet she almost looks gleeful.

"I found it!" Chet yells a few minutes later from the top of the ballroom steps. He lifts up a painting, and then hurries down the steps. It's a portrait of a man, probably wealthy, I guess from his gray receding hairline and pointed beard and the white sash crossed over his silken clothes.

"So." Chet smirks. "Looks like the torn countryside painting is yours, after all."

"Indeed," Madame says. "For what you hold, Chet, is King Henry IV of France. Once we tidy up this room, all will be as good as before. Or nearly. We are saved from Monsieur's wrath."

"This is ridiculous!" Mrs. Jones huffs, her face blotchy and red. "Are you insinuating I'd steal a painting, replace it with a French countryside, hide the original in my room, and then tell you where it was?"

"She's got a point," Bella says. "Why would she do that?"

Chet's dad steps in front of Mrs. Jones. "We should call the police."

"We were set up!" Mr. Jones shouts. "Can't you see that?"

The adults hurl accusations at each other. I stare up at the ceiling, trying to block out the shouting and curses. Are the Joneses responsible for destroying the ballroom? But they couldn't have, since they were at dinner the entire time. Weren't they? And the maid did say she had seen a ghost.

"Silence!" Madame practically screeches, raising her hands into the air. "No one is calling the police. If they come, they will only ask questions, which we do not need."

"Agreed!" Mom says.

Laughter echoes through the ballroom. Everyone whirls

around to spy the cook at the top of the stairs, hands on her hips.

"Protecting secrets, Madame?" The cook laughs again, her bulk shaking. "No more. I tell zee world about all who disappear from zis place." She jabs her forefinger at her chest proudly and then she smiles hauntingly at Mrs. Jones. "Police do not like zieves."

"Thieves?" Mrs. Jones looks appalled.

"You wouldn't," Madame says with a gasp.

"Good," Chet's dad says. "It's only right."

"Ah! Shan Valrose," the cook continues. "Paparazzi will be pleased to see you." She tosses her apron on the steps, lifts up her chin high, and leaves.

Mr. Parker's face pales. "Someone get her!" He takes off across the ballroom and up the steps. The rest of the adults join him in the hunt.

Chet, Bella, and I stare at each other.

"Is your dad *really* an actor?" Bella says.

"Is he *really* a spy?" I say.

"Do you *really* believe everything in the tabloids?" Chet says with a huff, and then he takes off as well, leaving the two of us alone in the darkness.

"This place gives me the creeps." Bella crosses her arms over her body. "Let's get out of here."

I give the painting a further inspection, then squint in the moonlight at the other paintings hanging on the walls. None of the other paintings is damaged. "Why would the ghost tear up this painting and not the others?"

"Maybe it has to do with it replacing King Henry IV's painting."

"You're right. He was the man both Gabrielle and Marie were in love with."

A shrill of icy wind gusts through the ballroom, whipping

chilled air across my face and stinging my nose. A gonging shatters the silence, vibrating down the hall and into the ballroom.

"Have you noticed that every time that clock strikes twelve, something strange happens?" I point out.

The clock continues to gong and with the sound, the wind gains in momentum, swirling about the room. We cling to each other.

"What's happening?" Bella's voice quivers.

"I think we're entering my fairy tale again."

"Promise me to never write anything horrible, scary, or unhappy ever again."

I can't answer. I'm too occupied with the elderly lady's portrait before me. The eyes on the lady move. Then her nose twitches.

"Did you see that?" I whisper. "That painting moved."

The head slowly turns so that the lady's beady eyes focus on us. Then with a roll of her eyes, the portrait sighs. She tosses her head so that her white ringlets flounce. It's a well-practiced head toss, and I'm guessing the lady has done her fair share of head tossing and eye rolling in her life.

"Good gracious!" the portrait says. "Whoever let the Word Weaver in? Scat! You are not allowed here."

Those words seem to wake all of the portraits in the room. Their eyes rove to focus on Bella and me, shivering from the near arctic chill permeating the room. The portraits rumble and grumble in dissent over me being here.

"Go back, Word Weaver," they chorus. "Go back."

"We should do what they say," Bella says.

"But how? Besides, we can't help Gabrielle if we just run away. We need to figure out what to do before we leave in the morning. This might be our last chance."

Then, as if merely speaking her name has summoned her, Gabrielle drifts from the wall and starts gliding across the ballroom along a crimson carpet that appears out of thin air. A single white rose is clasped in her hands. She still wears the ball gown I saw her in the other night with Chet, but this time her hair has fallen out of its clasps and tumbles over her shoulders and down her back.

And there at the other end of the carpet stands a cloaked figure holding something, but I'm too far away to tell what it is.

Music fills the room, a melancholy tune that reminds me of how I felt after losing my big championship soccer game. Gabrielle floats along the thin carpet as if heading down a wedding aisle. With each step, a petal drifts from the flower to the floor, and as it lands, it bursts into the air as if exploding. The particles freeze midair, creating an icy trail behind her.

But when the last petal loosens from the flower, it's as if everything slows down. The music stops. The portraits scream in horror. And the cloaked figure holds something out to Gabrielle.

I break into a full-out run across the ballroom. I don't know why, but I have watched and read enough fairy tales to know that when the last petal falls, it can't be good.

Being a backup goalie taught me how to dive and protect. This was why I didn't think twice about flying through the air, or consider how it might feel to land on a tiled floor rather than the turf of the soccer field.

The petal hits the floor.

Ice bursts into the air.

And before I can touch Gabrielle, the princess vanishes.

26

Detectives for Dummies *Tip of the Day: It is
essential to record, catalogue, and organize all evidence
taken from a crime scene.*

Bella and I don't stick around the ballroom for another
second.

"Are you sure you're going to be okay?" Bella asks. "That
was some fall you took."

"I should've know better." I cradle my arm as we head
down the hallway. "I saw the petal fall. I should've known I
wouldn't make it there in time. What was I thinking?"

"It's not your fault. You were just trying to help her out."
Once we hit the hallway, Bella stops me. "Hey, sorry for not
believing you earlier. I should've known you'd never lie to
me. I guess I was upset that you and Chet were having fun
together."

"No," I say. "Don't be sorry. You're my best friend. No one
will ever replace you. I wish that all of this was a joke. But
unfortunately it's not."

We head outside in search for my mom. The butler stands
by the front doors, holding one of them wide open as if he
doesn't know which way the guests want to go.

Outside on the castle steps, Mr. Parker's—or is it Shan
Valrose?—booming voice argues with Mrs. Jones's wiry

one. Mom isn't anywhere in sight. I have so many questions swirling through my mind. What I need is peace and solitude to organize my five-million questions zinging about in my head.

After I tell Bella I need some quiet time to sort everything out, and I get to my room, I pick up my journal and pencil. But the blue glow beams from the pocket of my suitcase.

The pen is calling to me.

I clench my fists, fighting the need to touch the pen. Maybe if I write a new ending to my fairy tale, everything will be fixed. I know how dangerous the pen is, but what if I just touched it? For a second. To feel it's magic flowing through me.

And yet, a voice inside me warns that it's too dangerous. I hear Bella's echo begging me to never write anything horrible again. What if I ended up writing something bad? When I hold that pen, it's as if my deepest, darkest desires surface and come to life.

Suddenly, the room feels too hot and the walls seem to close in on me. Slowly, inch by inch, I back away, unable to take my eyes off the glow. It takes all my willpower to step out of the room. And then I flee.

I'm running down the stairs, slipping into the library, hoping no one will follow me. Tonight I need to be alone and figure out how to dispel the madness I've created.

A fire has been lit, spurting off sparks and casting twisted shadows on the floor and walls. The room has a woodsy smell to it, reminding me of campfires, a distant memory from my elementary school years at summer camp.

Since there aren't any other lights on, I drag a wingback chair closer to the fire with my good arm. The oak wood in the fire snaps and pops. I take out my notes and frantically start writing down all the thoughts scrambled in my head.

Journal Entry: Day 6 of France Trip

THURSDAY (JEUDI), 9:10 P.M.

Things are becoming really crazy here at the castle. Here are some of my latest observations:

1. *Chet's dad looks just like an actor named Shan Valrose.*
2. *Maybe he doesn't just look like Shan Valrose. Maybe he really is Shan Valrose.*
3. *Why did Chet and his dad lie about their name? Should I trust Chet?*
4. *Who did Chet's dad email the other day?*
5. *Mr. and Mrs. Jones bought a painting today. It was discovered on the ballroom floor torn to shreds.*
6. *The ballroom has been ransacked.*

—Suspects? Mrs. Jones (it was her painting, but she was at dinner the whole time), Mr. Jones (said he had a business call and hurt leg, which delayed him), and the ghost.

—Witnesses? Maid, said she saw a ghost (note: question maid about what she saw).

—Synonyms for ransack: loot, scour, raid, rummage through

*** The princess in my story has vanished!!!!!

There's relief in writing down my thoughts. I rest my journal in my lap and lean my head against the back of the chair. Tears edge the corners of my eyes. I'm so confused, and deep down inside, the world feels wrong. Like it's warped, and yet no one even notices or cares. The worst part: This is all my fault.

"There's something terribly wrong here," I say.

"Perceptive girl," a man's voice says in a thick French accent.

I scream and jolt into the air. My nerves are already on high alert as it is. A dark form of a man leans against the desk.

"Who are you?" I backtrack toward the door. "Where did you come from?"

"Don't be scared, Keira. I don't mean you any harm. In fact, just the opposite. I've had my eye on you ever since I sent my men to deliver you some food. We thought we'd made a mistake in thinking your mom was the one. And then you went and wrote that charming little fairy tale."

He knows about our break-in. He's responsible for the break-in. I'm so scared I can hardly move.

"I don't blame you for being scared. Ghosts appearing, a ballroom desecrated, the cook making threats. But then I don't blame Gabrielle, either."

Creepy Man is talking about the ghost like he knows her! I swallow my fear and continue retreating until my back presses against the door. I fiddle with the doorknob but can't turn it with my hands shaking so hard. Why could I be so calm and collected with ghosts, only to fall apart at a human?

"Who *are* you?"

"Please, take a seat," Creepy Man says. "I have a proposition for you."

The doorknob turns. Finally!

"It has to do with who *you* are."

My stomach drops. "What are you talking about?" Only, I do know.

"You'll want to sit down for this. Trust me."

27

Detectives for Dummies *Tip of the Day: Don't
blow your cover and tell anyone you are a detective.
Not even your cat.*

Creepy Man has my attention now. I plunk down on the chair.

"First, let me introduce myself properly," Creepy Man
begins, rubbing his clean-shaven chin. A watch glows on his
wrist. It looks just like the one the men who ransacked our
house wore.

The man strolls into the firelight, and I get a closer look at
this intruder. He's wearing all black, which is probably how
he blended in so well in the darkness. The mock dress shirt
buttons neatly to his chin and black shiny shoes glisten in the
flicker of the flames. Even his brown hair is slicked back to
perfection and his mustache curls neatly at each end.

"My name is Monsieur Monteque." He twirls his mustache
and gazes into the fire. "I work with a group of esteemed colleagues from the Historical Correction Organization. We
make sure things *progress* as they should in our history."

I can't think of how people could make sure history played
out in a certain way. This guy is bad news.

"So you're the castle owner," I say skeptically. "Madame
talks about you a lot."

"Does she, now? Yes, I do own this lovely castle. Came
into ownership not too long ago, actually. If you look at the

history of Chenonceau, you shall see it has been a coveted castle. Even the king of France, King Francis the first, yearned
for it. So much so, he stole it from its owners using back taxes
as an excuse."

I stand, pretending my legs aren't shaking. "I've heard all
this already. I should be going."

"But then something terrible happened," he goes on,
ignoring me.

"Terrible?"

"Or perhaps wonderful?"

"That doesn't make sense." I don't like his tone. There's an
edge of a threat to it.

"As of last January, history was altered," he says.

"The past can't be changed. That's impossible. And if it
could, there is no way any of us would know if it had."

"Remember when I said I'm a part of a group of colleagues?
Trust me when I say we have a device that notifies us when a
new story has interwoven with a story from the past to alter
the course of the present."

"I don't understand."

"Basically, we believe someone rewrote Chenonceau's history. Historical records now say that four hundred years ago,
a duchess was murdered here by her stepsister."

Suddenly, it's hard to breathe. He knows who I am, what
I've done. But my mom said to say nothing, tell no one. I need
to divert the attention off myself.

"You're talking about my story, aren't you? You think I
copied the castle's story and made it my own to win the contest. But you have to believe me that I had no clue about any
of this until after I got here."

"Oh!" Monsieur picks up *Girls' World* magazine. It flaps
open to the page where my story is printed as the winner of
the *Happily Ever After Contest*. "You mean this little story?"

"I don't understand the problem."

"I must not have been clear. There is no problem. This is our solution. You are our solution."

Okaaay. This guy is delusional. "I am?"

"Indeed. I believe there is more to you than you can possibly know. You have a talent, my dear Miss Harding, and this story proves it. When you wrote this fairy tale, your story connected with an event from the past, wove itself through it, and changed history."

My pulse hammers against my skull and my stomach churns so hard I'm pretty sure I'm going to throw up. He knows about the Word Weavers! One thing I do know: There's no way I trust him.

"Okay, I admit it," I say, ramping up my lie. "I cheated. I went into the history book and took the story from there and rewrote it, tossing in a few fun words. It wasn't exactly like the original story, but it was pretty close. Does that mean I'm disqualified from the contest?"

"Come and look at this."

Then Monsieur slips on a pair of spectacles, pulls out a manila folder, and starts laying cards, photos, and printed schedules onto the desk next to my story. I inch closer, realizing with dread that he has hard evidence. Creepy Guy knows about everything that has happened at the castle this past week, including every excursion I've been on, the ghost sightings, and the disappearances.

"How do you know all of this?"

"Like I said. I own this castle. And I make it my job to know everything about the events within it. Everything in your story is exactly as history tells us it went." He peers over the top of his spectacles and narrows his eyes at me. "And according to your story, a ghost captures someone every Friday when the grandfather clock strikes midnight, which has happened at this castle ever since you wrote the story."

"Someone has gone missing every Friday? Why hasn't anyone done anything?"

"As soon as our device alerted us that a historical event was interwoven with a new story, we began searching for the source. I rushed to France to buy the castle and close its doors. If it hadn't been for me, we would have lost a terrible number of poor souls. I made sure no one entered the castle until two weeks ago to prepare for your arrival. The library was customized just for you, in fact. I also made sure you had the best desk France had to offer so our Word Weaver could be royally inspired. It is unfortunate about the poor maid who went missing last Friday, but it just couldn't be helped."

"That's horrible!" I say, aghast.

"Tomorrow it will be Friday once again," Monsieur says. "And this time, I will be here to watch the events unfold. I've made sure the ball will proceed as planned to follow the specifications of your fairy tale. The events on Friday will prove that you are what I believe you are. A Word Weaver."

"This is all pure coincidence. Nothing more."

"And if you are indeed a Word Weaver, then I kindly invite you to join my colleagues and myself in our endeavors to change history for the good of all mankind."

I stagger backward, desperate to escape those intense eyes. A new thought races through me. Monsieur is the very person Mom said we had to escape from.

I need to find my mom. It's time to get on that first flight out of Paris.

*Fact of the Day: Chances of a comet hitting the
Earth in the next one hundred years? .001
(even though there is no actual record of such a
comet ever hitting the Earth).*

*Chances of a Word Weaver existing and changing
history—obviously better than a comet.*

FRIDAY (VENDREDI), JUNE 18TH

The next morning is a flurry of activity as two trucks rumble
down the once quiet path of the castle and begin unloading all
of the equipment for the ball.

I stride out of the castle, rolling my suitcase behind me.
Sure, I am early, but after last night, I couldn't leave soon enough.
Bella is already outside, where she's meeting Cheryl to help
instruct the workers on where to put the objects and on the
unpacking of the tables, chairs, and decorations. I find Bella
on the bridge, waving her hands as she yells out directions.

"Isn't this so amazing?" Bella says when she spots me. "I've
always dreamed of planning my own event, and now it's really
happening!"

"Bella." I hate saying this. "We have to leave in an hour to
catch the train to Paris. I told you that last night. Tell me
you're all packed."

"Are you sure we have to leave? Nothing bad has happened. I mean the whole thing with the ghost was scary, but it's just a ghost. She can't hurt us. Besides, how can I leave all of this?"

A worker passes by, teetering a glass statue of Cinderella's slipper. "Hey, don't break that," Bella warns the carrier. "That's the centerpiece. If it breaks, the whole experience won't have the complete effect."

Last night when I told Mom what Monsieur said, she went into a complete panic and started cleaning her entire bedroom. We ended up deciding that I would continue pretending I had no idea what he was talking about. Since he seemed to want me for his historical organization, Mom didn't think our lives were in any jeopardy. Then the next morning, we'd slip out of the castle and catch our train to the airport without telling anyone except Bella.

I just hadn't counted on Bella not wanting to come.

"You have to trust me, Bella. We need to leave. Please."

"When has the ghost hurt any of us? And you saw her yesterday walking down the aisle. She needs us more than ever. We can't leave now!"

I laugh. It comes out like a nervous, freaked-out kind of laugh. "Oh, no. The ghost is the last thing I'm worried about right now. It's Monsieur."

"Oh, yes! I met him this morning. He seemed kind of weird, but nice enough. Hey! Not that way; the tables belong inside the castle, not in the gardens!"

I plop down on the top of my suitcase and groan while Bella reverts to organizing the delivery for the ball. How am I going to convince her to come with us?

If only I could tell Bella the truth about who I am, but Mom forbade me. She said if Bella knew the truth, it could put her in even greater danger. And that in itself tears my heart apart. The gravity of the situation pulls at me, and I don't know if I can hold up under the weight of it.

Now I understand my mom's need to keep secrets. Now I understand the lies.

*　　*　　*

I rush back upstairs to find Mom. Maybe she can convince Bella we need to leave, even if I can't. The only problem is, Mom isn't in her room. And not only that, her suitcase isn't even packed! What happened?

Then I spot a note on the dresser. It's addressed to me.

> *Dear Keira,*
>
> *I have decided I was being foolish and overreacting to not allow you to attend the ball with Bella. Therefore, I canceled our tickets, and we'll be flying back to Florida at our original date. I'm being taken to a fantasy bookstore to buy stacks of wonderful novels before we leave.*
>
> *Have fun today and I'll see you tonight at the ball.*
>
> *Love,*
> *Mom*

I read and reread the letter. Why would she do this? It doesn't make sense! I toss the note aside in frustration. This was her idea, and after talking to Monsieur, for once I agreed with her one hundred percent. Something isn't right.

*　　*　　*

I march downstairs to find Bella to tell her the news. At least somebody will be happy. But back outside, I find only the

Dragon, wearing a designer black pantsuit with a thick silver choker, speaking with Mrs. Jones.

"Cook quit?" Ms. Teppernat says in a shrill voice. "The little beast. Someone should have stopped her. Now what will we do?"

"Oh, we thought we had stopped her from leaving," Mrs. Jones says. "But this morning she left a note saying she quit. She must have snuck out. Can you believe it? It's quite shocking."

"Well, it's no matter. I suppose I'll just put the caterer in charge of the banquet. That cook was zany anyway."

Then her eyes fall on me. "Keira! Whatever is the meaning of this suitcase? Bella says you two are leaving within the hour!"

"Change of plans," I say. "We're staying until Saturday morning as planned. I was confused."

Maybe this is a good thing, I think. Maybe this will provide a way for me to save all of the people who had been vanished or even murdered. There's still time for me to figure out a way to save Gabrielle and whomever the stepsister decides to kidnap and take to the Dark Tower tonight.

When I finally find Bella and tell her, she throws her arms around me. "Thank you! This ball means so much to me. I'm so excited, but nervous, too."

"It's going to be completely perfect." I squeeze her hand.

"Don't ever think of scurrying off on me." Ms. Teppernat wags her finger at me. "Now, hurry along and change into the dress Cheryl has picked out for you. Or did you forget to look at your revised schedule? Today's your boating trip with the mermaid theme."

"Oh, I had nearly forgotten!" Bella says. "There's just too much to do for the ball setup."

"I don't want to go by myself," I say, but in reality what I want to do is sit down and figure out a way to solve this problem.

"Don't worry." Chet's voice comes from somewhere above us. "I'll tag along. I've been bored out of my mind all morning."

We all look up to find Chet rappelling down from the balcony above.

"I guess you can come." I narrow my eyes at Chet. "But only if you promise to tell me the truth about your dad."

"Saints alive, get down from there at once!" Ms. Teppernat says. "And the boating trip was designated only for the girls as part of their package. But I suppose if Bella wants you to take her place, I could allow it."

"Awesome!" Chet practically free-falls the rest of the distance, but surprisingly lands next to us with practiced ease.

29

Detectives for Dummies *Tip of the Day:*
If your investigation dead-ends, look at it from a
different viewpoint.

Cheryl changed me into a medieval-style dress. The top is sea green with a black corset secured around my stomach using a ton of intersecting strings. Then the ocean-blue skirt flows to my ankles and a matching bow is tied to the back of my hair. My face has been dusted with green and blue sparkles to portray a "mermaid glow" according to Cheryl. Chet and I follow Ms. Teppernat and the two camera guys down the path, all the way to the pier. Just ahead, two rowboats bob in the water. Ms. Teppernat's cell rings as we reach the dock.

"Unbelievable," Ms. Teppernat says. "This better not be a problematic call."

She answers the call in her usual perky, sweet voice. Then her eyes bulge. She presses the phone against her shoulder and tells Chet and me she'll be just a moment.

"WHAT?" she screams. "That is completely unacceptable! I refuse to take no for an answer." She paces the pier, her heels clicking against the wood. "I can't work under these conditions. A wandering ghost, no cook, a destroyed ballroom, obnoxious kids. What next?" She stops mid-stride. "YES! The ball is tonight!"

She throws her phone into the river and rattles off a string of really bad words.

Chet and I clamp our lips, not daring to speak. Even the camera guys look uncomfortable.

"Everything is a disaster!" she says. "It's as though I've been cursed!" I cringe, hating that word. "Tonight has to be perfect," Ms. Teppernat continues, now focusing on Chet and me. "My job is on the line here. Do you think you can manage that?"

"To be honest," Chet says, "perfection and I don't really mix well."

"Um," I say, all the while knowing the odds of tonight being a disaster are very high. Like maybe a one hundred percent chance. But Ms. Teppernat looks as if she wouldn't mind breathing fire and scorching us alive, so I figure it's always best to keep the Dragon happy. "Yes, I'm confident it will be perfect."

"Well." Ms. Teppernat smooths out nonexistent wrinkles from her suit and clears her throat. "I may have gotten a little carried away. You two have a nice boat trip. The camera crew will follow you in the second boat. Be back at the castle after lunch. I'm going to deal with the madness that awaits me."

I don't want the ball to go perfect for Ms. Teppernat. I want to find a way to keep someone from getting taken by the ghost tonight. Not only would I be able to save Gabrielle, but then it will also prove to Monsieur that he's wrong about me being a Word Weaver. Even if he isn't.

Ugh! So much is riding on me fixing everything. If only I knew how to stop the disaster.

After Ms. Teppernat storms away, Chet and I hop into one of the boats, me holding my skirts so I don't trip, and push off from shore, each holding a paddle. The camera guys take the second boat.

The castle emerges into view as we make the turn in the river. Seeing it, so beautiful and perfect, when in reality I know it's haunted, only saddens me. This is all my fault. How could I have let this happen? I study each window, thinking about the different rooms, each already holding a memory. My eyes scan the roof.

"Chet." I squint harder at the roofline. "Remember when we went up into the attic?"

"Yeah."

"Weren't there only three front windows and two side windows on this side of the castle?"

"Maybe. But I wasn't really paying attention."

"Look at the top floor to the left of the turret. There's a window I never noticed before because the only way you can see this side of the castle is from the river."

"So you think there is another room up there?"

"Yes! The room on the far side has to be the one that was lit up when the Pegasus flew me by the castle. When we went up there before, I was so focused on discovering the missing objects that I didn't consider the room I saw with Pegasus could be hidden."

"We should check it out."

I study him. Can I trust him? What is the truth behind him and his dad?

"Is your dad really an actor?" I begin as I dig my oar into the water. "And if so, why is he pretending he's not?"

"Okay, truth time." He sucks in a deep breath. "Yes, my dad really is Shan Valrose. And yes, he really is an actor."

My oar pauses mid-stroke, surprised at his admission. "Wow. And what about working as a spy?"

"That's true, too. Although I didn't realize it until the other day when we were at the Internet café. I saw Dad's email and put the pieces together. Apparently, that's why we're on this trip. So I asked him. When you guys came in, we were having a fight about it."

"So your dad is an actual *spy* and was sent to watch us?" I say, putting the pieces together. "That's horrible. Not only are you liars, but you were paid to lie to me."

"You gotta believe me. He says it's like acting. But hey, you call yourself a detective, right? How much different is that from spying?"

"It's completely different. Besides, its not acting if you're living out real life. How can I trust anything you say now?"

Chet paddles some more, quiet now. That excited, wild look that's usually plastered all over his face has vanished, leaving only emptiness.

"It was Monsieur who hired him, wasn't it?" I say.

"How did you know?"

"Lucky guess."

My stomach turns. Not because the water is starting to get rough, but because this is how it feels to be betrayed.

It's all now clear how Monsieur knew the details of what had been happening at the castle and with the ghost. Chet told his dad, who in turn told Monsieur. The betrayal felt like someone stabbed me in the chest. I scrutinize Chet, still unsure if I can trust him.

"Listen," Chet finally says. "I've never had real friends before. Everyone always wants to be my friend because my dad is a famous TV actor and we are rich. And here I had the chance to be normal and for you to like me just because of me."

"That makes a lot of sense," I snap. "You hang out with Bella and me and act like you're our friend when you're really sneaking around and telling all of our secrets to your dad and Monsieur? That's not what a friend is."

"Yeah, I get that. But this is the first time Dad's ever taken me on one of his trips. We finally got to be together, even if this place was boring at first. And when he gave me the spying assignment, it seemed really cool and it wasn't hurting anyone. For the first time since I can remember, my dad and I had awesome talks.

"But you're right. It was dumb of me to think I could make friends *and* have a dad who wants to hang out just for fun."

"It's not that, Chet," I say. "You're a cool kid. Even if your dad is some famous guy. You don't need to pretend to be someone else to make friends."

"You really think I'm cool?"

"Yeah, except when you're spying on me."

"Listen," Chet says. "Give me a second chance. I really want to help you with this ghost thing. Let me prove to you that I'm doing all this as your friend. Not actor kid or spy kid."

"I'll think about it."

I wonder what it must be like to always be trying to get your parents' attention. I had the opposite problem. My parents are excessively protective and noisy. I hide things like my writing utensils and novels from my parents. While Chet goes to extremes to get any attention from his dad.

A heavy wind blows across our faces as we float down the river Cher. In the distance, a gonging sound echoes. That couldn't possibly be the grandfather clock in the castle, could it? My pulse quickens. The boat shifts and dives down a small dip in the river. I set my paddle aside and clutch the edge of the boat to keep myself from falling overboard. But the waves are becoming too strong and my oar flies into the river.

I glance back to see where the camera guys are, but it appears they are stuck in a bramble of fallen trees. They're digging their oars into the water and arguing.

"Don't worry." Chet hunkers down and pushes his oar into the water to keep us from crashing into a massive rock ahead. "I've got plenty of experience with river rapids. At least on my Outdoor Adventures video game back home."

"I don't think Ms. Teppernat knew this river had rapids," I say. "And why didn't we think to wear life jackets?"

"Life jackets?" Chet's voice trembles slightly for the first time since I met him. "Yeah, maybe that would've been a good idea."

Whitecaps build up along the tips of the water's surface. Our tiny boat tosses about along the river that has become a frothing surge of water. As the waves crash against the rocks, the water sprays into the air, reminding me more of glitter than water. The water crystals almost hang above us, as if transforming before my eyes, sparkling like stars.

"Something is wrong!" I have to shout over the surging waves. "Paddle to the shore."

"I'm trying! The current won't let me."

Then the water before us bursts up like a geyser. Chet's paddle is ripped away by the wind. We cling to the sides of the boat, barely able to hold on. The water drops like an endless waterfall, with our boat hovering at the precipice. The geyser's center opens up and a horde of fish fly out of it. But these aren't just normal fish. Their mouths widen, revealing jagged teeth. Snapping with hungry jaws. The air fills with the sound of barking.

"Ahhh!" Chet screams. "Piranhas!"

A gleam inside of the boat catches my attention. Strapped to each side is a sword. My fingers fumble to release one from its bindings.

"Chet! Get your sword!"

He glances back. "What are you talking about?" I toss him the jewel-hilted one. He snatches it out of the air like he's been fencing all his life. "Hot fire!"

"Remember when I wrote that story in my room and you said you wanted to be a pirate with a jeweled sword. I think this is my story coming to life."

He slashes at the oncoming monster fish. "But I didn't say anything about piranhas!"

Finally, the other sword is free, and I grip it tightly in my hand. At first I'm not sure I even know what to do with it. But when a flying fish sails through the air, eager to take a chomp out of me, I slice the air in a perfect arc, severing the fish in half.

"What's up with the rowboat?" Chet says. "Next time, make the pirate boat be a ship. A big, giant one. With a glass case to keep these suckers out."

"How about next time don't mention boats or swords or pirates. It's too dangerous!"

Chet and I fight side by side, wobbling back and forth in the tiny rowboat, desperately trying to not fall in. One of the fish clamps down on his arm. The teeth are razor sharp, digging into his skin. He yowls out in pain. I don't hesitate. I stab the fish in the eye. Its jaws release their hold and it flops about on the boat. I kick it overboard.

"Fire and smoke," Chet says. "You saved my life."

I cut the air, slicing the last of the fish in half, and shrug. "More likely your arm."

And then all is silent, other than the churning of the waves. I'm about to sit back on the bench and attempt to use my sword for an oar when the center of the geyser bubbles up again.

"Uh-oh," Chet says. "Tell me I didn't ask you to write about a sea serpent."

From the depths of the river rises a massive sea serpent. Its green scaled skin glitters like emeralds stitched together. Its body is wider than our entire boat. It slithers around us, slipping in and out of the water like it's playing hide-and-seek. Sharp spikes peak up along its back all the way to the giant tail fin. An eye blinks, assessing us, while it flicks its tail into the water, causing massive splashes and sending our little boat tossing and churning.

"Next time you write a story, I promise, promise, promise I won't mention sea serpents," Chet says. He's holding his sword bravely, but his legs are shaking.

"Next time?" I laugh hysterically. "I don't think there will be a next time."

"Word Weaver," the sea serpent says. I'm so shocked that it can speak, I almost miss its next words. "You should not interfere. Danger lies ahead if you do."

"But what if I have to?" I yell back, coughing from the spray of water that gushes around me. "The princess will be taken to the Dark Tower and the vanishings will only continue if I don't do something. And if the story happens as it's supposed to, then some really bad people will take my mom and me away."

"There is only one way to proceed," the serpent says, voice rumbling like thunder. "Yet it is a perilous risk. Things of the past must be made right."

The serpent's long, spiked tail beats against the water's surface, causing the boat to be flung into the air. Perhaps he meant for us to go flying back to land, except that's not what happens. I claw at the edge of the boat, desperate for its solidness.

But all I find is empty air.

My body plunges into the water and I sink down, down, down.

Darkness fills the river and slices off any glimpses of sunlight from the surface. I kick and grope, hoping to find the surface or even the bottom of the river. But I don't. Then I remember the advice from my camp instructor. If you fall into water and you can't figure out where the surface is, just allow your body to naturally float upward.

So I steady myself, waiting. My lungs are exploding. Panic floods my senses. I have only seconds left.

*Safety Tip of the Day: When boating, always wear
coast guard—approved life jackets. Do be sure to check
that your life jacket fits snugly.*

My body is hauled up to the surface, as if an unseen hand has
grasped me and dragged me up. I inhale the air, drinking it in
with huge gasping gulps. Then I swim through the semi-
darkness until I'm able to touch the ground with my feet.
Splashing through the water, I emerge onto a stone-surfaced
floor and collapse, not caring that half of my body is still
lying in water.

My body shakes so hard from the near-drowning experience that it takes some time to gain my bearings. Every muscle
aches from being tossed about. Finally, I drag myself out of
the water and slog to the shore.

I almost died back there. And that brings back all the memories of me being pulled into the ocean's undertow outside my
grandma's beach house. If it hadn't been for the lifeguard who
came out to save me, I'd have drowned.

Back at the house that day, Grandma made me a cup of
cocoa and a slice of spice bread.

"There, now," Grandma told me when I couldn't hold the
tears back anymore. "You had yourself a little adventure,
didn't you?"

"I wish I hadn't. Reading and writing about adventures is far better. And safer."

"Perhaps." Grandma pressed her lips together as if she was trying very hard not to say something. Then she shook her head once and patted my hand. "Sometimes it's what we take away from our adventure that makes us stronger. Don't be afraid of those tears of yours. They mold us and transform our endings into something meaningful."

Someone coughs not far away from me, the sound echoing off the stone walls and pulling me back into the present.

"Chet?" I'm hoping it's him and not some other horrible creature. "Is that you?"

"Yeah," he says, still hacking away. Through the dim light, I make out his outline as he staggers to his feet. "Man, I thought I was going to die. Maybe that was a little too close to living on the edge. Next time, let's wear life vests."

"No kidding."

"But the sword, nicely written."

"Thanks. I think."

We are in a cavern with stalactites jutting down like teeth. The pool we emerged from laps against a stone floor. How had we gotten inside this place? It must have an underwater passage-way or maybe it was just magic. The near darkness suffocates me. The only reason I can see anything at all is because of the white dots on the far stone wall providing some illumination.

"Those look familiar." I slog my way to where the dots are scattered on the wall.

"They are the same kind of dots that we saw in the tunnel outside of the kitchen," Chet says.

"Which means this place is somehow connected to the castle."

The line of glowing white dots along the edge of the cavern leads us to a staircase.

"Should we follow the trail?" I say, peering into the dusty, cobwebbed tunnel. The horrible bugs from the last tunnel trip are still branded vividly into my brain.

"It's either stick around here until you die of hunger, or follow the trail." Chet says. "I'll go first and pave the way through the spiderwebs."

I don't argue about that. The stairs twist up like a funnel, around and around, taking us higher and higher. The walls feel as if they want to swallow me, and I imagine every bug I've ever seen might at any second pop out of the gloom and land on my nose.

Soon the tunnel breaks into a fork. We argue over which way to go.

"Definitely right," Chet guesses. "Left will take us to the same boring tunnel we were in before."

"But at least we know we'll get back to the library," I say because I'm sick of being in soaking-wet clothes.

"What if this way takes us to the attic?" Now Chet has my attention and he knows it. "You said you wanted to see if there was a secret room in this place."

"Fine," I mutter. "But there better not be any spiders."

As we scramble through the tunnel, new thoughts haunt me. "What do you think the sea serpent meant by 'Things of the past must be made right'?" I wonder out loud.

"That you've got to fix the problem. Not sure how helpful he was, nearly killing us only to tell us something that you already know."

The passageway twists and turns in the strangest ways. There are times it's such a narrow squeeze that I'm not sure how any adult could have fit in this place. We pass another fork in the tunnel. To the left is a thin wooden door with an emblem of a tree on it. I've seen that before. This is the section I ran through with the princess!

"Keep going up," I say. "We're getting closer to my bedroom."

Chet doesn't ask how I know this. We keep shuffling along, when Chet slips and falls forward, and of course I fall after him. We tumble down the set of stairs, rolling over each other. I plop on top of him at the bottom. Chet grunts in pain.

"Apparently, there are steps down as well that I forgot about," I groan, trying to stand. My hand catches on something sharp. It feels gritty, like rusty iron. "I think I found something."

I yank down on the bar, and at first it moves only slightly. But when I shove all my weight into it, a grinding sound rumbles above my head, like ropes moving through a worn-out pulley. The wall slides open, flooding the two of us with light.

"Smoke and fire!" Chet says. "How did you do that?"

"I have no idea. But it's the Joneses' room!"

I squeeze through the passageway's new door and enter Old Mother Hubbard's lair. Fortunately, they aren't there. The floor creaks under my weight as I sneak through the room. The clock reads thirty minutes to twelve, which explains my growling stomach. The book of ghost stories lies open on the table by the bed. And Mrs. Jones's binoculars hang on a nail by the door, obviously returned.

"What are you doing?" Chet says, hanging back in the passageway. "This is their private room!"

"Hush! I'm sleuthing, of course!"

"And here you were saying how mad you were that I was spying on you."

"But they're not my friends and you are."

"Does that mean we're still friends?" Chet asks.

My foot trips on something sticking out from under the bed. I fall, making a huge thumping sound. Chet shushes me while I look to see what tripped me. A long metal bar juts out beneath the bed. I pull it all the way out and examine it. It's a simple tubelike pole. What would they need a metal pole for?

A shrill laugh explodes in the hallway. A key scrapes in the door's lock. My eyes widen.

"They're coming!" Chet whisper-yells to me. "Get back here!"

The door handle turns. I dive back into the wall, my skirts tangled up in my legs, but I manage to slam up on the lever. As the passage wall closes shut, the bedroom door opens and Mrs. and Mr. Jones stride into the room, talking about the ball.

"Did they see you?" Chet whispers.

"I don't know!" I press my ear to the wall, listening.

"I don't believe it!" Mrs. Jones says, but it's a deeper and stronger voice than I remembered her voice being. Fortunately, the wall must be quite thin because I can hear every word.

"That idiotic Teppernat woman isn't canceling the ball. And how come Renee is quitting? Maybe we didn't pay her enough. Our plan isn't working."

I sit up straighter realizing why her voice sounds different. She's speaking with an American accent, not British as she was before.

"Stella," a man's voice, sounding very much like Mr. Jones, says. "You *need* to stop the panicking. Tonight is our night. We stick to the plan. All will go as it should."

"You need to go back and offer her more money. There are going to be loads of people and a camera crew there tonight. This is our opportunity."

"She's a scullery maid. How was I to know?"

Chet shifts beside me, kicking up dust. He sneezes. And then begins sniffing as if he's going to sneeze again. I slap my hand over his mouth just before he does.

"Did you hear something?" Mr. Jones says.

"I'm sure it's only those two troublesome girls next door,"

Stella says. "Good heavens. That Keira is far too nosy for her own good."

"Naw! I wouldn't worry too much about her. She's just a kid."

"Of course. You're right." There's a slight pause. Something slams. A drawer maybe? "I think I've got everything. Do you have the poison?"

Another pause, and then Mr. Jones says, "Do you really think we should do this?"

"Don't be ridiculous! We agreed. My vote is for the punch."

"What if I get thirsty?"

"Stop acting like a baby. Oh, dear. Look at the time. Do you think the bank closes at noon?"

"Let's not risk waiting," Mr. Jones says. "Come on, I have the keys."

After some more shuffling and drawer slamming, the room falls back into silence. I wait for another minute.

"Let's get out of here," I whisper. "Keep moving forward. I think my room is next!"

As we struggle down the tunnel, all I can think about is poisoned punch and haunting ghosts. My stomach tightens.

A few steps later we hit a dead end. Chet kicks at the stone in the bottom corner just like he did when we entered the library. The wall slides open and we stumble out into my bedroom.

"How did you know this would lead to your bedroom?" Chet asks as he dusts himself off.

"Because I've been in that passageway before. When the ghost grabbed my hand to escape something that was chasing us, she took me that way."

"That sounds so completely crazy, but I believe you. Do you think the Joneses are going to try to kill us?"

"I don't know. But one thing I do know is we should definitely not drink the punch tonight."

31

*Fact: The youngest kid to climb Mount Everest
was thirteen years old.*

"Do you still have the key?" I ask Chet.

"Why? Are you going into the attic?"

"No, I'm just going to carry it with me all day." I toss my hands in the air. "Of course I'm going into the attic! You saw what I saw in the boat. There has to be a secret room up there. And I'm going to find it."

"Then I'm coming."

"No, you're not. Because you would tell your dad and Monsieur everything and ruin my entire existence."

"I'm not going to tell them. I swear. Cross my heart. Hope-to-never-climb-Everest kind of swear."

I give him a hard stare. "Never-ever-climb-Everest?"

"Never-ever if I tell."

"Fine. But if you do, I'll write a story about you being scared of heights."

"I can live with that deal."

Back in front of the attic door again, Chet fishes the key from his pocket and slips it into the lock. We head up the creepy stairs, where I immediately run to the front room's side wall.

"There has to be another room behind this wall." I slide my hand across it. "Do you think Monsieur knows about the secret room? Maybe he's hiding something?"

Chet looks skeptical. "Keira, it's a wall. Besides, there aren't any doors behind it. How would anyone get back there?"

"Maybe there's another secret passageway that we haven't discovered yet," I say as I inspect each crack. "Or maybe this is all just a crazy idea of mine and the place doesn't exist."

Meanwhile, Chet puts his ear to the wall as he pounds on it. "It does sound different. Maybe there is something on the other side."

Footsteps clomp up the stairs. I search for a place to hide, but that's kind of pointless since the room we are in is completely empty.

"Don't bother hiding," Madame's voice calls out from the stairwell. "I know you're up here." She enters, a scowl on her face. "What are you two doing? This is restricted territory."

I step toward Madame. "From the river, I could see a window in the castle tower. But as you can see, there is no entrance to that room in the castle. So where is it?"

Her eyes take in my wet clothes and hair and then Chet's. "You two look like drowned rats." She presses her forefingers together in a triangle of sorts. Knowing my luck, she's running through her curse list, deciding which ones to use on us. *Don't turn me into a spider!* I think, but all Madame says is "It doesn't exist."

"And you expect us to believe that?" I say.

"The last window is purely ornamental. Behind the glass is brick."

"You're lying," I say.

"Don't believe me?" Madame laughs. "Then go to the library and study the architectural designs if you must. And I'll be taking back that key you're holding, young man."

Disgruntled, Chet passes over the key. After we are marched back to the second floor, she locks the door. *Bummer.*

"So much for finding answers," I mumble. "We only seem to get more questions."

32

Decorating Tip of the Day: You, too, can be a
decorator! Always remember—less is MORE.

I leave Chet to search for my mom. When I reach her room,
she still isn't back from her shopping trip. What is going on? I
check the closet only to find her purse is still there. Mom
never went shopping without her purse. And that meant she
wasn't really shopping. I recheck her note. This time a partic-
ular line sticks out.

> *I'm being taken to a fantasy bookstore to buy stacks of*
> *wonderful novels before we leave.*

Specifically, the part about Mom buying stacks of novels. She never, ever reads novels and especially wouldn't go
to a fantasy bookstore. It is one hundred percent, no question, absolutely forbidden in our house, plus she detests
anything of the sort. Now that I know about my family's
ability as Word Weavers, I understand her reactions a little
better. But still. She wouldn't go out and buy novels. Which
means:

> *1. Mom is trying to send me a message.*
> *2. Something horrible happened to her.*

The only person who would want any harm done to my mom is Monsieur.

*   *   *

After changing into dry clothes, I scour every inch of the castle, looking for a hint of Mom or Monsieur. Hours later, I come up with nothing, so I head to the ballroom, where Bella is knee-deep in gold material. Surrounding her are leafless potted plants strung with white lights, and boxes of small clear teardrop bulbs.

The room is packed with workers, hanging long swaths of tulle from one end of the ballroom's ceiling and then dipping once again to the other end.

"How's it going?" I plop onto the floor next to Bella. "This place looks more like a construction zone than a party zone."

"Great now that the cleaners have left after sweeping up all of the glass. The only bad part is the windows aren't quite as pretty as they once were."

"At least no one was hurt," I say with relief. "Have you seen my mom today? I can't find her anywhere."

"Didn't you say she went shopping?" Bella pins a portion of the material to one of the long tables to create a table skirt.

"Yeah, but she didn't bring her purse, and she always takes that with her when she shops." I fidget with Mom's note and then finally hand it over to Bella. "Read her note and tell me if I'm crazy to think she's disappeared."

Bella reads through it and shakes her head. "She says she's going shopping. Maybe she put her money in her pocket. You know how criminals prey on tourists. I know you don't want to hear this, but I think you're a little paranoid. But then, after this week, I'm wondering if we're all a little paranoid."

"There's something in the note that's nagging me. Mom said she was going shopping for fantasy novels. You know how my mom hates all things fictional, right? Do you think it was a clue?"

"Maybe." Bella stands and brushes golden dust off her hands. "Or maybe she's just out having fun shopping in France, which sounds way more likely. So what do you think about this table? It's the first one I finished."

Shimmering golden material covers the circular table with one of the leafless trees resting on top. White lights weave through its branches, and tiny clear teardrop globes hang from its boughs. Electronic tea candles are scattered around the tree.

"We'll light the candles just before the ball begins," Bella explains. "The decor is to be chic with a romantic flair. What do you think?"

"I think it's completely magical. Now I see why you didn't want to leave. I'm so impressed you designed all of this."

Bella beams.

"But it looks like you still have a lot of work to do," I say. "Let me help you out."

We work together for the next hour, but as I'm stringing the lights on one of the trees, the words from the sea serpent bounce back and forth in my mind.

" 'Things of the past must be made right,' " I whisper, trying to make sense of it.

"What did you say?" Bella says.

"Made right," I repeat again. "That's it!"

"What's it?"

"What if it's a play on words? Like he meant *right* as in w-r-i-t-e. What if I rewrite the story? Rewrite it to be obnoxiously happy. You know, *write* it *right*. The ghost would be appeased, Gabrielle and all those who have been vanished would be saved, and Monsieur would leave my mom and me alone because it would prove we weren't who he thinks we are. Then I could have my life back. Problem solved."

"Okaaay," Bella says. "I have no idea what you are talking about, but it sounds like an impressive plan."

"I have to go do something." I jump up and hurry out of the ballroom.

"Where you going?" Bella shouts after me.

But I don't stop. As I rush up to my room, I make mental notes of how my new story should be written. I will become a writer again.

But this time as a true Word Weaver.

*   *   *

I don't waste a second. After shutting and locking the door, I dig out my magical pen from its latest hiding place under the mattress. Then I sit down at the desk overlooking the river and pull out some of the loose-leaf paper inside the desk. I'm going to write a new version of my fairy tale.

For a brief second I hesitate, swallowing away the doubt lumped in my throat. Because when I write something, things don't always work out as I expect them to. Like the piranhas and the sea serpent.

"Please work, please work," I say in a whispered breath.

I touch the pen to the paper and stroke out the word *the*, but the page remains blank. Frowning, I shake the pen a little, waiting for the "magic" to spark from it. To feel the rush and the power that this pen evokes. But there are no streams of blue or whooshes of wind. I grit my teeth and scratch out the word *the* again. Still nothing.

I drop my head in my hands and groan. This isn't the time for writer's block.

Why won't the pen work? It's so not fair.

There must be something wrong with the ink, I think. Maybe it's run out. I open the desk to find a drawer full of writing supplies. Pencils, papers, notepads, ink pads, inkwells, quills. The options are endless. I think about Monsieur telling me he created the library and ordered this desk just for me. He probably planted all of these writing materials here, too. Sneaky man.

I pull out the inkwell, unscrew the top, and dip my finger into the ink bottle. My fingertip is now black. I smear the ink off my finger and onto the paper, leaving behind a black trail. Satisfied the ink works, I dip my magical pen into it.

I don't care if my pen is ruined. All I care about is Mom and Bella and all the people who are being affected by my fairy tale.

Once the pen has ink on it, I draw a sweeping line across the journal. But not even a smear of ink spills onto the paper. It's as if the pen is purposely soaking up the ink. Not even a scratch marks the paper. I bang my fist against the desk and then furiously scribble all over the table with the pen. Not that it matters.

Because the pen doesn't leave a single mark.

"This can't be happening to me!" I yell. "I won't allow it to happen."

But deep down, I feel—no, I know—that my fairy tale is real and Mom's warning how it can't be changed is the truth. My scalp tingles as reality sinks in even deeper. *An evil ghost who locks people away forever was created by yours truly.*

I stare at the silver pen, which at this moment looks like an ordinary calligraphy pen. But every time this pen works, I don't get writer's block. The story comes to me like—like magic.

That thought settles into the pit of my stomach, and every-thing tumbles into place. When I wrote that unhappily ever after fairy tale, I created a magic world. Once made, it couldn't be unmade. This is what Mom had meant. Maybe that's why every time I entered my fairy-tale realm, the creatures kept telling me I didn't belong there. A painter doesn't live in her own painting. A sculptor doesn't become his statue. And a writer isn't supposed to live in her own books.

Everyone told me this except Pegasus. The memory of seeing myself in the room in the attic of the castle prickles at my mind. I had been writing in a large book on a floating desk with the words flying into the air like golden dust.

Madame must be lying. That secret room and book exists. And I need to find it.

*Rock Climbing Performance Tip: Keep your center of
gravity close to the wall you are climbing.*

It's more than an hour before I find Chet. He's climbing out
of the fireplace from the secret passageway in the library.
Cobwebs are strung across his chest, and his shirt looks more
gray than black.

"There you are," I say. "I've been looking everywhere
for you."

"You have?" Chet's eyes brighten. "You don't hate me
anymore?"

"When you're being my friend, you're actually a pretty
cool guy. I need your help. I need to go through the secret
passageways and see if I can find one that leads to the secret
room in the attic. But you have to promise me you won't tell
your dad about this."

"Promise. But I just got out of the passageways." Chet
shakes his head. "Went back in with a flashlight. There's no
passageway that leads to the attic. But I was able to retrace my
steps to find the one that goes to your room!"

"Don't you dare ever use that entrance again! Understood?"

"Uh, yeah. Absolutely. Never again."

"There has to be a way to get to that secret room." I pace
the floor. "We just haven't thought of it yet."

Chet sticks his hands into his jeans pockets and stares off at the bookshelf. Then he grins. "There is one way."

"Why do I get the feeling I'm not going to like your idea?"

"You won't. But if you really want to get to that room, you'll do it."

*   *   *

We dart past the film crew that's piling into the castle's main hall, sneak past Ms. Teppernat, who is yelling at the new caterer about incompetence, and then skirt past the butler, who does in fact see us but as usual says nothing.

Chet leads me to the right of the entrance, finally stopping at a long rope that streams down from the roof to my feet.

I turn to face Chet. "You can't be serious."

"Hey, you said you wanted to get to that window. Yesterday, I already did the hard part by scaling to the roof and securing the ropes. This is what I've been doing in my spare time. All you need to do is climb up. Think of it as rock climbing."

"I've never rock climbed. I'm scared of heights. What if I fall?"

"You won't because I'm going to tie you in and then I'm going to belay you. If you fall, the rope will catch you."

"You want me to trust an eleven-year-old boy with my life?"

He cocks his head to the side, thinking, and then says, "Pretty much."

"Oh my stars." I shake my head as I realize I'm really going to do this. I'm that desperate. Annoyed, I snatch the harness Chet's holding out for me. "I can't believe I'm going to do this."

The harness cinches tight around my thighs and waist like an awkward seat belt. Chet hooks the rope through a belay and then clips the rope to his own harness.

"Will this really hold me?" I try to keep my voice steady, which is pretty much impossible.

"Yep," Chet says. "You're actually wearing my dad's harness. I was bummed he was going to be too busy to use it, but it's come in handy after all."

After we're all hooked in, Chet gives me a quick lesson on how to step into the crevices within the stones and how to press my body closer to the rock to keep my center of balance.

"Don't sweat it, though, if you fall," Chet says. "I'll catch you with the rope."

"I'm going to fall?" I gulp and stare up at the distance between the ground and the tower window. "I don't know if I can do this. I don't know if I even should do this."

"Sure you should." Chet grins. "This is going to be *awesome*."

I press my palms to the castle wall and close my eyes. Faces flash through my mind: Gabrielle, Monsieur, and Mom.

It's through these images I gain the confidence to take the first step up onto the castle's brick. I pause, hovering maybe a foot off the ground. I didn't fall! So I lift my left leg and step into another crevice. One after the next, I climb higher until I'm dangling from the top of the windows of the first floor.

"You're rocking it, Keira!" Chet encourages me. "Keep going."

But then I slip. My fingernails scratch across the castle surface, and I feel myself falling. I scream. Suddenly, the rope snags and I stop falling. I'm dangling and bouncing off the side of the castle like a string puppet.

"See," Chet says. "I got ya!"

My breath heaves in and out so strongly I'm frozen. What a silly idea this was! There has to be a better way.

"Let me down," I call to Chet. "I can't do this."

"Sure you can. Just focus on the window."

I roll my eyes but grip the side of the castle and start climbing again. I follow Chet's advice and keep my eyes on the prize. Soon I'm nearly at the third floor. I am almost there!

Below, voices are yelling and screaming. I know I need to keep my eyes up, but I decide to check out what the commotion on the ground is about.

A group of people have formed where Chet is belaying me. It's easy to spot the flaming red hair of Ms. Teppernat. But then I also make out Bella, Cheryl, the Joneses, and Mr. Parker. Even a group of photographers who came to shoot tonight's ball are there. I squint against the sun's rays. It looks like they're taking pictures of me right now. And filming me, too!

Dizziness washes over me now that I'm looking down. The ground swirls. My fingers loosen their hold, and once again I slip. I drop a foot or so before the rope tightens, keeping me from falling. My heart still nose-dives.

Below, Bella screams and Ms. Teppernat screams at Chet, "Let Keira down this instant!"

I bite my lip. I don't have much time before Chet might break under the pressure he's getting. Focusing on the rounded lip in front of me, I grab hold of it and scamper onto the small edge until I'm able to stand up. I'm nearly at the window ledge!

One more climb up onto the next ledge and I'll be there.

Grunting, my palms slap against the windowsill's flat surface, and I haul myself up so that I'm sitting on the window ledge. A light wind blows my hair. I dare a glance out at the world beyond the castle. The view steals my breath away. The geometric-design gardens stretch out in a rainbow of colors, the river flows lazily beneath the castle, and the woods roll out in never-ending greenery.

But as I stare back into the window, my heart sinks.

Just on the other side of the glass is a stone wall. The same color as the ones on the outside of the castle. Madame was right. There's no room inside. It's a false window.

Survival Tip: If you end up locked in a tower, it's handy to bring a rope along.

"That was the most ridiculous, irresponsible thing you could ever possibly do!" Ms. Teppernat says the moment my feet touch the ground.

I don't have anything to say. In part because I'm too busy trying to stop my hands from shaking so I can unclip myself from the ropes. But mainly because all I feel right now is defeat. The window had been my last hope. I have no ideas left.

"You are grounded from rock climbing indefinitely," Mr. Parker tells Chet, and then takes the harnesses from him. "Don't even dare think of touching a rope until you can prove you are able to do it."

"But you saw her," Chet says. "I taught her to climb a castle. That's pretty cool, if you ask me. And look, she survived without any injuries!"

"Thanks, Chet, for helping me," I say. "You were a great teacher."

"It's private property," Ms. Teppernat says. "If Monsieur found out, we'd be kicked off immediately! Come along. The sun is setting and it's past time for you to get dressed."

We all turn to head back inside, only to find Monsieur there, twirling his mustache with his blazer flapping in the wind.

"*Bonjour, mademoiselles* and *monsieurs*," he says. "I see you have taken up a new hobby, Keira. Quite an impressive feat, if I do say so myself. But personally, I think you should stick to writing. It's far more exciting than climbing castles, is it not?"

"Huh?" Chet says. "He has no idea."

"Where's my mom?" I say, sick of his pleasantries. I wish I could write that grin off his face in my next story. "I know you've done something with her!"

"I haven't the slightest notion what you are speaking of." Monsieur shrugs and then clucks his tongue as if I'm some naughty child. "But perhaps your little story can help us solve this problem. Let me see here."

He whips out a copy of my fairy tale from his pocket. Slowly he unfolds it and holds it tight to keep the wind from snatching it away. "Ah, yes," he says. "Here is the line:

"*On the night of the ball, the queen discovered the truth about the stepsister and confronted her. But the stepsister was too clever, even for the queen. With a swish of her magic, she vanished the queen to the tallest and loneliest tower. Nothing would stop the stepsister from fulfilling her destiny tonight at the ball. She would make the prince see that they were destined to be together. No matter what it took.*

"Perhaps your mom and the queen have something in common, yes?"

"We don't have time to sit around and read Keira's fairy tale," Ms. Teppernat snaps with a scathing glare. I'm amazed fire didn't burst from her mouth. "The ball begins in less than an hour and she still isn't ready. So if you'll please excuse us."

But I can't move. Is Monsieur right? Had my fairy tale somehow intertwined with my real life and taken my own mother? Suddenly, it's too hard to breathe. It's too much to take.

"Wow," Chet says. "That stepsister sounds like pretty bad news."

"That's the whole point." Bella rolls her eyes. "It's supposed to be a parody of fairy tales, right, Keira? Keira? Are you okay?"

"I think she's going to faint." Chet squats down in front of me, peering intently at my face.

Hands direct me toward the front of the castle, but all I can see is Monsieur standing there, holding my fairy tale, a grin plastered on his thin face.

Party Planning for Pros *by Sleeping Beauty: When
planning a ball, do be careful whom you invite and,
more important, whom you don't invite.*

"Now, don't worry your pretty little head about a thing,"
Cheryl tells me as we start inside. "Your mom is perfectly
okay. I just saw her earlier. She said she had to work on your
departure plans."

"She did?" I grip Cheryl's arm tightly, and she begins nod-
ding vigorously. I want to believe Cheryl's telling me the
truth. She has no reason to lie to me, right? "That would be
something she'd say."

"That's right." Cheryl's face brightens as my steps grow
stronger. "Come along, and hurry so we can get dressed for
the ball. Your mom will be there, I'm sure of it."

Encouraged, I rush with Bella to our room to change. I'm
sure that I completely overreacted with Monsieur. I've been
so uptight ever since those burglars ransacked our house that
I'm making this issue bigger than it really is.

After Bella and I bathe, Cheryl presents our dresses to us. I
press my hands to my cheeks. It's so beautiful. The strapless
gown brushes the floor as I walk. The pale gold material
shimmers like a blanket of diamonds. Once Cheryl finishes
my hair and jewelry, she allows me to look at myself in the
mirror. I've never put much thought into my looks before, but

tonight I am beautiful. My skin glows in the setting sun, and my blue eyes sparkle. Then I spin in a circle, and my dress puffs into the air like sunbeams. Cheryl has tamed my brown curls to ringlets that cascade over my shoulders. A diamond tiara glitters on top of my head. A smile creeps over my face. There's no doubt. Cheryl really converted the two of us into princesses.

"Be careful with your crowns," Cheryl tells Bella and me. But Bella is so busy squealing and spinning around that I'm not sure she hears Cheryl. "They are on loan from the local jewelry store."

But even as beautiful as the dress and the crown are, it's hard to let myself be whisked away in what should've been the most amazing moment for me.

Tonight the ghost is supposed to return and take another person. The Joneses are planning on spiking the punch with poison, and my mom still hasn't shown up. The biggest problem is that everyone is too busy to care about any of this. Except me.

My heart beats faster. Somehow, I have to fix all this, I think as I play with the soft folds of the dress. I've never been so nervous in my life—even when I tried out for the soccer team.

Cheryl ties a large golden bow around my waist and flounces up the skirt of the dress one final time. "There. Now, don't you look just like a princess?"

"It's the most beautiful dress I've ever seen," I say. "Thank you."

If only I had written my fairy tale with a happy ending. Sure, I had been mad at Mom, but I never wanted anything bad to happen to her.

Bella practically floats over to me in a dress that reminds me of puffy blue clouds. Her brown skin glistens with jeweled undertones. "Isn't this heavenly?" she says, humming softly. "It's like a dream."

Or nightmare, I want to say, thinking of what tonight may hold. But I don't, because this is the moment Bella has been dreaming of her entire life.

Instead, I hug my best friend, saying, "Bells, you look like a fairy." Then I frown, remembering the fairies that bit me on the forest path. "No, actually, you look far prettier than any fairy."

"Really?" Bella smiles. "You, too. I know you're worried about tonight, but will you try to have fun for me, please? All of my work will be showcased and photographed for the world to see. It's a big deal."

"Of course," I say, feeling guilty for nearly forgetting about Bella's big project. "From the parts that I saw, it will be amazing. Maybe you'll even get attention from some of the big design colleges."

"Put these on, Keira." Cheryl hands me a pair of sparkling white heels.

"Heels? I don't think that's a good idea. I'll trip for sure."

Cheryl insists, but when her back is turned, I slip on my indoor soccer shoes for good luck. We step into the hall, and Cheryl turns off the light. From the corner of my eye, a blue glow emanates from under the mattress of the bed.

The pen.

I want to turn my back on it. To leave it behind and glide down the stairs to enjoy a fairy-tale ball. But a trickle of sweat pours down the sides of my face. My hands shake. And I know I can't. I can't leave the pen behind. I need to hold it. Keep it safe.

"I'll be right back," I tell Cheryl and Bella. Then I pick up my skirts and dash into the room. I clip the pen inside the sash of my dress. An electric spark courses along my palm from the pen. Maybe this pen isn't totally bad, and it's giving me good luck. I could use all the luck I can get.

* * *

I lift my dress and practically float downstairs, feeling like a true princess. Music and the sounds of laughter waft up the stairs, and a sliver of nervousness cuts into me. Standing in front of the ballroom doors, I find Cheryl, still wearing her apron over her purple sequined ball gown; Bella; and Ms. Teppernat.

Tonight the Dragon is decked out in a tight pink dress with sparkly feathers ringing her neck like a collar and a long train that sweeps across the ground behind her. Her eyes appear huge due to her fake sparkle lashes and the gobs of fuchsia eye shadow.

"Ah!" she says. "Don't you both look marvelous? Now let's go over the instructions. You must follow these exactly or everything will be ruined. You will both enter together and curtsy. Remember to pause at the top of the stairs, count to ten, and smile for the cameras. Then continue walking down the red carpet—do remember to glide with your chin held high—and commence directly to the dance floor for your dances."

"I really don't want to go in until I see my mom," I say. "Have you seen her? She said she'd be back by now."

"Oh, dear." Ms. Teppernat wrings her hands. "I, um, think I did, actually. Didn't you see her slip into the ball just a few minutes ago?" she asks Cheryl, who pauses from readjusting Bella's dress. Cheryl's eyes grow large, but her mouth remains shut. Perhaps because she's clamping a bunch of pins between her lips.

"Yes, I believe we did!" Ms. Teppernat answers for Cheryl. "Now, don't worry about a thing. It's going to all be simply magical."

Bella squeezes my hand as we step up to the front of the ballroom doors. "Don't worry, Keira. I bet she's right and your mom is already inside."

The double doors swing open, and I'm stunned by the huge crowd staring at us as we walk in. Bella slips her arm through mine as we take our first steps. Flashes of light spark around us like lightning. The thunderous sound of people clapping echoes through the ballroom. My knees lock up even though I know I'm supposed to curtsey.

"For heaven's sake, smile for the cameras!" Ms. Teppernat barks behind us. "It's not *that* difficult."

I scan the crowd from the top of the stairs. There must be nearly a hundred guests, not including the film crew. Earlier, Cheryl explained that the citizens of Chenonceaux had been invited for the event, as well as some French celebrities.

Somehow, I manage to bow, and I attempt to smile. Finally, the camera flashes cease and a buzz of conversation starts again.

There's no doubt that Bella nailed the decorations. The golden tables scattered about the room shimmer from the white lights on the trees and tea lights. The white tulle sweeps across the wood-beamed ceilings. Banners hang along the walls displaying pictures of different fairy tales. White rose arrangements adorn every table.

"The decorations look really great," I tell Bella as we step down and follow the red carpet.

"Glide!" I hear Ms. Teppernat whisper-yell from behind us by the doors. "Chin up! Smile!"

But then I freeze mid-stride. This runner looks exactly like the one Gabrielle walked along just yesterday. The memory of the white petals falling to the floor and bursting into icy clouds rushes over me.

"What's wrong?" Bella says, studying me hard. "Let's go get some food. I see a massive stack of cream puffs that are calling my name. Plus, I want to make sure Cinderella's slipper isn't melting."

Then I spy Chet. He is standing there on the left, hands behind his back, all dressed up in a smashing tux. When his eyes catch mine, he winks and peels back a lapel of his black jacket to reveal his hockey jersey hidden underneath. I crack a smile.

"Wow," Chet says as he saunters up to Bella and me. "You guys look really—pretty." Then his whole face gets red.

I point to his jersey. "Nice jersey. It really adds a lot to your tux."

"I take it the jersey wasn't Ms. Teppernat–approved." Bella lifts an eyebrow.

"Yeah, she's been too preoccupied to notice. Um, Keira," he says, and starts looking everywhere except at me. "I left the rope up for you just in case. Thought it might be fun to sneak out and climb to the roof later."

"Nobody is climbing any roofs tonight." Bella clamps her fists onto her hips. "You guys really scared me earlier."

"Thanks, but the window isn't really a window. Just a fake."

Then, as if sensing we were talking about her, the Dragon swoops in before we can escape to the pastries.

"Time for the waltzing!" Ms. Teppernat says in her sing-song voice.

"You're not serious?" I eye the swarm of photographers who are surrounding the dance floor. It's one thing to dance in a room with just an instructor. But it's another whole thing to dance in front of a hundred people and be filmed.

"Completely," Ms. Teppernat says. "Just make a few moves. Enough for the photographers to get a shot or two."

"Okay." I bite my bottom lip. "But after that, I need to go and look for my mom."

Chet moves to stand before me, saying, "Let's do this thing. Then we'll go find your mom." He smiles and the knot in my shoulders releases.

"Right." I place my right hand in his and my left on his shoulder just like we practiced. "Thanks."

He reddens a little, but says, "That's what knights in shining armor do, right?"

I think about him in that knight helmet as the string quartet begins playing. "Honestly, I think you should stick to climbing. It fits you better than that armor."

As we dance, my stomach flutters. Not that horrible sickening feeling that I'm so used to feeling, but this time it's like a flurry of butterflies taking flight.

"Good thing that dance instructor isn't here," Chet says. "She'd be all over our moves."

"One, two, three, four." I mimic our instructor's voice, giggling. "I suppose we look more like toy soldiers than dancers."

Chet lifts my hand over my head and sends me into a spin. The crowd claps approvingly.

Halfway through our dance, Mrs. Jones skirts past me, wearing a dirt-brown floor-length dress. She beelines for the punch bowl, all the while making fugitive glances around the ballroom. My footsteps slow as I watch her. She withdraws a bottle from the folds of her dress, opens it, and then slips the bottle behind her while turning her back to the punch bowl. She pours the contents of the bottle into the bowl, all the while looking out into the crowd, smiling with a big goofy grin.

"Chet!" I whisper. "I just saw Mrs. Jones pour something into the punch bowl."

"Seriously? I didn't think she had the guts to really spike it with poison."

"Well, apparently she does. Come on, I need your help." I drag Chet over to the punch table as Mrs. Jones sashays away, nonchalantly patting down her white curls.

As soon as Mrs. Jones ducks into the crowd, Chet and I each take a side of the large bowl and lift it off the table. Punch sloshes over the side.

"Did anyone drink from it?" Chet says through clenched teeth, trying to balance the bowl.

"I don't know. I wasn't paying attention. What do we do with it, though?" My muscles complain under the weight of the bowl.

"I don't care." Chet groans. "Just as long as it's sooner than later."

"There." I nod to one of the plants. "Dump it in that."

Chet backpedals across the ballroom while I focus on keeping the punch in the bowl. We're halfway to the plant when Ms. Teppernat steps into our path.

"What in earth's name are you two doing?" Ms. Teppernat says.

"Saving the ball from disaster," I say.

"Saving the ball!" Ms. Teppernat scoffs. Her eyes narrow, thinner than the arrow slits of a castle. "Ruining it, more like. You look like hooligans lugging that punch across the ballroom floor. What are you thinking?"

"That maybe it was poisoned." I grunt. "If you'll excuse us, this is kind of heavy."

We skirt around Ms. Teppernat and dump the punch into the plant. It splashes over the planter sides, too much punch for the pot to handle, and pours out in dirt-mixed streams on the floor. The hem of my dress drags through the muddy punch. I try lifting my skirts, but it's too late.

"Don't worry," Chet says, as if reading my thoughts. "It's nothing that a good bar of soap won't fix. Besides, I think the sludge really makes the dress."

A group of guests huddles along the sides to watch us. Ms. Teppernat's features soften and an easy smile replaces her angry red-lined lips. "Don't worry, everyone. Keira and Chet will be returning to their dance within moments."

But when she turns back to speak to Chet and me, she speaks in a grinding, low voice. "If you dare ruin this ball for me," she says through gritted teeth, "so help me, *Girls' Life* will revoke all purchases made for you on this trip, and you and your mother will pay for every penny. I promise."

"Speaking of my mom." I cross my arms. "You know where she is, don't you?"

"Hush! You're making a scene." Ms. Teppernat attempts a smile and waves at some of the onlookers now taking pictures.

But I'm not finished. "I'm making a scene? I've done everything to help you make your little ball a success! It's the Joneses you should be worried about. They poisoned the punch and are ruining all your plans." I point to Mrs. Jones by the cheese platter. "There she is. Ask her yourself."

Mrs. Jones's eyes widen when she sees me pointing at her. A small crowd has gathered and are staring back and forth from Mrs. Jones to me. But Old Mother Hubbard's features smooth away from her face like a cleaned whiteboard. She waddles over to me and shakes her head, those white curls shaking as they like to do.

"I overheard your ridiculous accusations," Mrs. Jones says. "How can you accuse me of such a thing?"

"Because I heard you talking to your husband about poisoning the punch. And then with my own eyes I just saw you pour a bottle of liquid into the punch bowl!" A gasp erupts from the crowd. The room falls quiet. Even the string quartet in the corner stops playing.

I barrel on. "And while we are fessing up, admit that it was your husband who vandalized this room last night."

"Never!" Mrs. Jones presses her hands to her chest as if in shock, her eyelashes fluttering. Mr. Jones races to her side, and she leans against him as though she might faint.

"I found a pole in your room, under your bed," I continue, unimpressed with Mrs. Jones's theatrics. "It was the perfect weapon to break the windows with. No one suspected you at first because when the maid screamed, we had all been there together. But then after hearing your conversation in the bed-room about bribing the maid, I remembered. Mr. Jones came in late for dinner that night. He apologized, but what he was really doing was switching the paintings and destroying the ballroom. Then he paid the maid to scream during dessert, hoping we'd all have forgotten he was missing earlier."

Ms. Teppernat turns to face the Joneses, her face ashen. "Why is it that I believe her?"

"Total speculation!" Mr. Jones shouts, sweat dripping down his temples. "What you say is slanderous. I will sue!"

"You're a better sleuth than I thought, Keira!" Chet laughs. "That makes perfect sense. I remember that night clearly because Mr. Jones sat next to me. He did come in late."

"This is preposterous! We were set up," Mrs. Jones yells. "Why would we do such things? We're here on our second honeymoon."

"No, you're not," I say. "Back in January, some of your house staff started to go missing. There were all kinds of rumors about you, even that you killed your staff. You went bankrupt and had to sell your castle for a ridiculously cheap price. You're not even from England. You're American! That's why when you are alone, you speak with an American accent. I bet Jones isn't even your real name because you knew it would be listed in the house registry. But since the sale, you've never been the same and have blamed the hauntings on the new owner."

The Joneses glower at me.

"And now here you are in your old home, this very castle, trying to buy it back from Monsieur Monteque by making this place seem haunted so the castle will be more afford-able. You've been getting clues on how to make a house look haunted from that ghost book of yours. It was you who stole everyone's stuff, hid it all in the attic, and vandalized the ballroom."

This really gets a reaction from the crowd, especially with most being owners of the surrounding châteaus. People gasp and the murmurings grow into a loud buzz.

Bella pushes her way through the crowd, sliding her arm through mine. "Let's not forget about the hairnet."

"Good point, Bella," I say. "Mrs. Jones, if you'll excuse me, but I really must know." I reach up and snatch a handful of Mrs. Jones's white tresses. I yank it so hard that Mrs. Jones's hair comes off.

Her wig, actually.

Mrs. Jones shrieks, holding her hands to the hairnet that has slipped loose, releasing a trail of long brown hair. "Give me my wig back, you little devil," she snarls.

"It *is* a wig!" Bella says. "I love it when you're right, Keira."

Ms. Teppernat's mouth forms a giant O. Then her face contorts so that it becomes all scrunched up like a bulldog's. She slaps Mrs. Jones in the face. "How dare you try to ruin my ball?"

"How dare you try to steal my castle from me!" Monsieur's voice booms from the top of the stairs. Now everyone's attention is suddenly on him. The crowd whispers as he makes his way down the steps. "Regardless, your antics are meaningless. Because there really is a ghost who haunts these halls each night. No need for you to attempt to conjure one up."

But before he can say another word, the grandfather clock in the hall starts booming. *Bong! Bong! Bong!* The sound echoes across the room in a resounding drone. I clench my fists, counting each of the gongs. Because I know now that when it reaches twelve, it means my fairy tale has woven its way into our world. It's Friday. The night of the ball.

The stepsister's ghost will appear.

And someone will be taken.

*Cauldrons for Cowboys: For hearty outdoor cooking,
we recommend cooking in our cauldrons.
Your stew will never taste the same.*

A whoosh of cold breeze sweeps through the hall, blowing out nearly all the candles in one giant gust. Even the electric lights have stopped working. Without the lights, we're left with only a few candles and the moonlight that trickles through the tall windows, casting long, hollow beams across the ballroom floor. Everyone screams. But not me. I'm a stone statue. A chill creeps up my legs. The ghost is here. I can feel it in my bones.

"What is going on!" a man shouts. "I did not come tonight for some childish prank."

"Ghost?" a lady in a pink dress says, her voice quavering. "There are ghosts here?"

Ms. Teppernat laughs and clasps her hands as if trying to hold everything together. "Of course there aren't any ghosts here."

"Oh, no, Ms. Teppernat," Bella says. "There is a ghost here and Keira is trying to figure out how to get rid of it."

"Yep," Chet says. "Saw it myself. Whatcha going to do about it?"

"And according to Monsieur," I say, "someone disappears every Friday night."

"But that cannot be! People said it was only rumors!" the lady in pink says and begins fanning herself.

Suddenly, it's as if our words process in the guests' minds. The murmuring grows and the crowd shifts, edging for the exit. One lady shrieks as a gust of wind blows through the ballroom. She bolts for the door. Her husband races after her, calling her name. A buzz rises from the crowd, some demanding answers, while the press frantically continues to snap pictures of the scene.

Pink Lady obviously can't take it anymore because she faints, collapsing against the nearby table and landing in the castle-design cake. Cake splatters everywhere. On the guests, walls, decorations. Arms spread out, Pink Lady groans from the floor, on her bed of white cake and frosting.

Chet scoops up a finger-lick and tastes it. "Delicious!"

Mr. Jones tramps up to Monsieur, saying, "You are nothing but a lying, cheating scoundrel. Sell the castle back to my wife and me before things get worse."

"Is that a threat?" Monsieur asks, his thin eyebrows rising.

The arguments rage back and forth among the adults. Suddenly, Mr. Parker drops his drink and collapses to the floor. Did he drink some of the Joneses' punch concoction? I wonder.

"Chet!" I say. "Your dad! I think something is wrong with him."

The wind kicks up stronger, and the chandeliers sway under the gales until they loosen their hold on the ceiling and crash to the floor. Glass shatters everywhere and the guests scream, scattering like mice across the ballroom.

I push through the crowd pressing against me to search for the ghost. There's no doubt that the stepsister is here.

The shards of chandelier glass glow a midnight blue, radiating light across the ground like lasers. Then the pieces gather together, whirling through the air to form a funnel in the center of the ballroom. Piece by piece the shards meld until a woman forms, floating in our midst.

The ghost.

Her ball gown is a deep purple, shredded so that the torn pieces float about her in the air like ribbons. Strands of hair wave about her face, concealing her features so I can't make out who it is.

The ghost reaches out a long pointy finger. At first I think she's pointing at me, but I'm wrong. Because beside me, Bella starts shuffling toward the ghost.

No. *No!*

"Bella!" I seize her arm. "Stay with me. The ghost is dangerous."

Still, Bella walks with a strength I've never known her to have. My arms latch around her waist. My feet slide along the tiled floor as Bella unwaveringly marches toward the ghost.

"Somebody help me!" I scream.

But looking about the room, my heart sinks. Everyone is literally frozen in place. Mouths opened in screams, hands extended, and legs stretched in full-out sprints. They can't see or know this whole interaction is even happening.

The faces within the portraits begin mumbling, their lips moving incessantly. At first I can't make out what they're saying, but then as their voices grow louder, the words become clearer.

"Beware. Beware. Beware, Word Weaver," they chant over and over.

"Stop!" I yell at them while clamping my arms tighter around my best friend.

"Beware, Word Weaver," an old woman says from inside her frame on the wall. "You are not safe in your own fairy tale. If you are caught by your enemy, you will be stuck here forever or, worse, destroyed!"

"I can't let this ghost take my best friend. I won't!"

But Bella continues her rigid pace so that I'm dragged across the floor until we reach the ghost's feet, so close I could touch her bare toes.

A black cauldron materializes beside the ghost. Curls of purple steam rise into the air. The ghost dips a chalice into the bubbling liquid and holds it out to Bella.

"No, Bella!" I scream, clawing at Bella's hand as she reaches for the chalice. "Don't drink it. It's poisonous!"

But Bella's arm is an iron bar, stronger than I could possibly imagine. With her eyes glazed, she takes a sip. I can't stop screaming, my voice echoing throughout the ballroom in a wail. The chalice drops from Bella's hand, smashing to the floor in a thousand pieces. A whirl of wind circles all of us, soaring and gushing with the strength of a tornado.

My grip on Bella loosens. I'm not sure how much longer I can hold on. One by one my fingers slip from Bella. I fall to the floor in a heap of golden material. Bella's skirts billow about in a tangle of blue like a deadly storm off the seacoast, and her black hair whips across her face.

And then she and the ghost vanish.

"Bella!" I cry into the darkness. I'm alone, wretchedly alone.

Survival Tip: Never drink anything from a stranger.

I rise to my feet. The ballroom is empty; everyone from the real world has vanished. I must still be in my fairy tale.

Then the howl of the wolves startles the silence. Somehow in the back of my mind, I know that they are signaling the beginning of their hunt. The hunt for the Word Weaver who must be punished for trying to tamper with her own story.

The hunt for me.

The portraits open their eyes and begin whispering as if they, too, fear the wolf pack.

"Beware, beware, beware, Word Weaver," they say, their voices no louder than the rustle of wind cutting through leaves.

A sob escapes me as the full enormity of watching my best friend be taken away sinks in. My heart beats so fast I can't think straight.

There has to be something I can do. There has to be a way to stop this madness.

I dash across the ballroom, glad I opted for the indoor soccer shoes rather than the heels Cheryl had insisted I wear.

But once I enter the main hallway of the castle, my feet slow. Something is crashing against the front doors of the castle in hard, solid thumps as if it is trying to ram down the doors. Then the sound of scratching. The doorknob turns.

And the castle doors are flung open.

There at the threshold snarls a group of five wolves. Their teeth glint knifelike in the moonlight as drool drips from their snarling jaws. Their green eyes narrow in on me.

"Word Weaver," the wolf in the middle says. "So pleased you decided to come back. This time we will make sure you never leave again."

They dive into the hallway, straight for me.

I sprint up the stairs, careening around the corner into the second-floor hallway. I bolt for my room and slam the door shut, locking it.

The wolves smash against the door as if they hit it at a full-out run. I turn to assess the room. A single lantern is lit on the desk, flickering a friendly glow amid the gloom. There is nothing of Bella's or mine in here.

What if I rewrite the fairy tale in my own fairy-tale realm? Would that change everything? Encouraged, I throw open all of the drawers, hoping for paper. They're completely empty.

The door bends in, the wood finally succumbing to the onslaught. I don't have much time.

"Run, Word Weaver!" voices whisper from the figures in the tapestries.

I glance at the door. A splintered gash snakes down the door's center. A green eye of one of the wolves peers through, unblinking.

Holding back a cry, I seize the lantern on the desk and race to the fireplace. I stare at the area, trying to remember back to the time when I ran this way with Gabrielle. How did she get inside the fireplace? I rub my hands over and over my head. And then I remember.

I slam down the fire poker. The back of the fireplace begins to rumble open, and I dash inside just as the door crashes to the floor.

Stumbling, squeezing, and sprinting, I race through the

castle's secret passageways. The wolves gain on me, so close behind I can hear their heavy breathing. Still I run, a plan forming in my mind. I need to find my way back outside.

Finally, just ahead, I spot the old wooden door with the two *W*s carved on it. I push my body into overdrive and shove myself into the door. But the wolves are too fast.

A wolf flies through the air, clawed paws outstretched toward me. I swivel around and smash the lantern on the wolf's snout, shattering its glass. It rears back and howls in pain as flames lick across its shaggy fur.

I don't pause but heave open the door and slam it closed, praying it will take a long time for them to break this door down.

Then I race down one of the garden paths, panting and gasping for air. The moon hangs above, now at its fullest, bathing the castle in its eerie glow. The wind turns colder, as if the air itself is trying to stop me from running back to the castle. Still, I keep running, praying, wishing, and hoping that Chet's rope is still there.

But as I careen around the bend, I skid to a halt. Before me hovers the iridescent sapphire form of the ghost, still wearing her shredded dress and the hooded cloak that shrouds her features.

"Stepsister?" I whisper, my heart in my throat.

Another gust of wind blows across the garden, tearing back the ghost's hood. Red hair whips about like fire. I gasp. The ghost is Ms. Teppernat!

"Ah, yes, Word Weaver," Ms. Teppernat says, her thin lips gray in the moonlight. "Now you know the truth. I have you to thank for giving me so much power. It is through you that I have been able to live long after my days should have ended."

Ms. Teppernat appears so different with her long red hair hanging loose. Free of the hood, it whips behind her like a kite.

And those eyes! A horrible emerald green just like the wolves. They mesmerize me. My knees buckle and I drop to the ground. Ms. Teppernat raises her hand and squeezes her fist tight. Then, as if mimicking Ms. Teppernat's fist, my lungs squeeze so tight that it's as if all the air inside my head has been sucked up and I'm lost in the raging wind.

Ms. Teppernat loosens her grip and lowers her hand. My lungs gasp for air and suck it all in, choking uncontrollably. She laughs, a long ear-piercing laugh at me as the pack of wolves slink out of the shadows, flanking her.

"This has been delightful having a Word Weaver enter my fairy tale," Ms. Teppernat says in a hollow voice. "How did I ever get to be so lucky? But the fun must end. You are getting rather tiresome, and I grow weary of your games. Come, give her the flower."

Another figure emerges from the trees. Madame! Slowly, she glides along the path, holding out a single white rose.

"You thought you were invisible," Madame says. "But you were no feat for us."

I attempt to stand, but my legs are locked. "You have my mom here, too, don't you?" When they both smile at me, I nearly lose it. "Where are my mom and my best friend?"

"Oh, those two?" Ms. Teppernat chuckles and then snaps her fingers.

A blue mist forms between us. The wind picks up and in my mind I fly toward a tall, twisted tower. As I draw closer, the two shutters at the top of the tower swing open, revealing a spiral staircase. Along either side of the staircase are cells. Prisoners clutch the bars that pen them inside, and their voices vibrate in my ears.

"Help me, Word Weaver," they wail. "Help me!"

My body continues on, moving up the Dark Tower, higher and higher, past prisoner after prisoner, until I reach the very peak.

And there sitting in piles of hay are Bella and my mom.

"NO!!!!!" I yell, leaping to my feet, fists clenched at my sides.

The mist vanishes, along with the tower and my loved ones.

"And now you know the way of things," Madame says, blowing the flower petals around me. "Do not worry, little Word Weaver. There is nothing you can do. They are scheduled to be killed shortly. Just as soon as I am finished with you."

"Please." I'm desperate. How can I save them? "This wasn't supposed to be real. It was just a story. I had no idea it would actually come true! I'll do anything to fix this!"

"Fix this?" Ms. Teppernat gasps as if I suggested she eat toads for breakfast. "There will be no 'fixing' happenings in my fairy tale, Word Weaver. This is how you wrote the story. This is how the story goes. I had heard that Word Weavers at times feel sudden regret for how their stories turn out and try to change events and such. I will not have such nonsense. It is completely unacceptable."

I back up, scanning the area for a way of escape, but the trees fade into blurry images and my legs and arms are numb.

Meanwhile, Ms. Teppernat snaps her fingers again and her cauldron and chalice appear from thin air. She holds the chalice out to me. A coil of steam curls upward.

"Time for a little drink, my dear Word Weaver," the Dragon says in a singsongish voice.

The chalice floats right beneath my lips. I can't think of anything except drinking the liquid. An overpowering urge washes over me. I must drink it! My thirst begs me to take a teeny, tiny sip.

But a burning sensation in my hip yanks me away from wanting to drink. Instinctively, I reach down to my waist to stop whatever is burning me. My fingers curl around my magical pen.

Everything crystalizes before me as I grasp hold of the pen. I'm not thirsty. And I definitely don't want to drink from that cup. Angry, I plunge the pen into the chalice. The green liquid bubbles up.

An explosion bursts from the chalice, it's filled with gunpowder. The power of the explosion hits me. I sail across the garden and land in a row of bushes.

Not waiting for the black haze to dissipate, I dash through the bushes and continue my race to the castle, crossing my fingers that everything I wrote with my pen really does come true. Finally, I stop beneath the very window I tried to get to earlier today with Chet.

A glistening glow radiates from the window at the peak of the castle. It's the only warmth in this whole land. And there, swaying lightly in the evening breeze dangles the rope that I had written about when Chet and Bella had me see if the pen truly worked. I want to burst into tears with joy. For once, my pen has worked in my favor! The rope's rough strands bite into my palms, still scratched and rubbed from climbing the castle earlier.

The window is an eternity away. Could I climb that high with the rope again? It's one thing to rock climb, secured with a harness and someone belaying me in case I fall, but quite another to just climb a rope. The image of Bella and Mom locked in the tower springs to my mind. I take a deep breath and begin climbing.

The wolves come bounding around the castle just as I reach the first-story window. My heart jams into my throat. I haven't climbed high enough yet. As I expected, the lead wolf gallops down the path and leaps up, snapping at me.

I plant my feet on the castle, lean back, and scale hand over hand up the wall. One step after the next, I make my way up, straining against the pull of gravity and the fiery ache of my muscles. My skirts threaten to trip me, and twice I hear the rip of material. If there was motivation to climb before, I sure have it now.

At the second-story window, I wrap my body around the rope, resting my arms, and dare a peek below. Like before, the ground swims, but this time my friends aren't below but the wolves, circling the rope as if dancing, are.

I nearly throw up. "After today, I'm never, ever, climbing anything again," I promise myself. Heights and I aren't a good combo.

I count to five, and at five I force myself to start climbing again. Not once do I look down. Instead, I focus on the golden light. This time as I pull myself up on the window ledge of the top turret window, there's no stone wall. It leads into a room. I understand now. This hidden room only exists in my fairy tale.

YES!

I slide open the window and scramble inside, falling to the wooden floor with a resounding thud. I'm so thrilled that this place exists and I found it, I practically kiss the dusty floor.

*How to Write a Book 101: A book must have a
beginning. And a middle. And an end.
Otherwise, it simply is incomplete.*

As if in a trance, I stare at the room laid out before me. This is like the control room of my fairy tale. Cobwebs string from the rafters to the corners of the room. Dust cakes the floor and walls.

But I can focus on only one thing: the massive open book on the desk in the center of the room. Golden light streams out of it, flows across the air, and out the window.

I pad across the room with only the sound of my golden dress swishing to fill the silence. The book is flipped open to near the end of the story. One word at a time bursts aglow like the flames from a fire, shooting off sparks into the air. Then that word becomes as black as coal. As if it's written in permanent ink. Word after word blazes in sequence.

My pulse pounds as everything clarifies. When the words erupt into flames, it's as if they have taken life. As if they become reality.

The page turns.

All by itself. Magic is flipping the pages.

I scan the page, my heart beating so fast it almost blurs my vision. It's hard not to make the words twist and turn as I read them. Because there on the very last page of the book, written in my own handwriting is:

And they all lived unhappily ever after.

THE END

A gasp stutters from me and I stumble backward, needing to put space between myself and those words. They are my words. This is my story. My stupid, thoughtless, ridiculous story. Why did I write it with that ending? What was I thinking?

Trembling, I sag into the chair, rubbing the inside of my hands furiously as word after word flares to life. I have only a few minutes at most before the story comes to an end!

Mom and Bella's capture is my fault.

I need to destroy this book, just as this story has destroyed the lives of so many others. I pull out my pen and hold it up as if it's my magic wand. I start writing in the book. But just like those other times, nothing happens.

Frustrated, I grip the last page and pull and twist it. "Rip, you moronic page. You're supposed to rip!"

I keep pulling back against the book, leaning all my weight into the effort. Still it doesn't budge, and the words continue to appear. It's as if the book is made of rubber, bending and twisting, but never breaking apart. I scrunch up the paper toward the spine of the book, but when I release it, the pages cascade back into place.

My body trembles and my hands shake. I can't hold back the tears anymore. Taking both fists, I raise them above my head and swing them down, smashing them on the book with all my might. Over and over, my fist hammers the pages.

Then I pick up my magic pen, and holding it like a dagger, I plunge it into the whiteness of the book. Over and over, I stab the book with blind rage until my hair falls from its pins and strands of curls cling to my wet face.

It didn't even make a dent in the book! And my Word Weaver pen appears as sharp and shiny as ever.

But then a speck of ink disappears from one of the words. I squint, studying the page. Dozens of tiny splashes have dropped onto the pages and act like erasers, whiting out the words.

"They must be all the places my tears dropped." I say aloud. "But I don't understand why."

I hold my breath as more words vanish. Every place my tears touched, the ink washes away. That's when I understand. I can't rewrite the ending until the things of the past are erased. Only then can I make them *write* as the sea serpent told me to do.

The memory of my grandma's words after my scare at the beach rush back to me. *Don't be afraid of those tears of yours. They mold us and transform our endings into something meaningful.*

"That's it!"

Without wasting another moment, I lift up my Word Weaver pen once more. This time it's shining, and sapphire sparkles flicker out of its edge. A thrill shoots through me and I start writing, eager to create my new ending. This time the ink flows and imprints on the page.

"It's working." I'm breathless, exhilarated. "It's really working."

> *Princess Gabrielle, with the help of a mouse chewing through her rope bindings, escaped from the Dark Tower where she had been vanished. Then, one by one, she released all the prisoners the stepsister had imprisoned there.*
>
> *When Gabrielle and the queen returned home, they banished the stepsister from the kingdom and she was never seen again.*

Now that the kingdom was made whole again and no longer in mourning, Princess Gabrielle and the prince celebrated with a huge party that lasted a whole month, eating as many chocolate croissants and Twizzlers as they could muster.

And they lived happily ever after.

THE END

Mind Twister: All good stories must come to an end.
Even if they're only the beginning.

As soon as I write *THE END*, tiny specks of light sparkle on the pages. They radiate larger and brighter until the whole book beams in a brilliant golden glow. The light swells until I'm forced to cover my eyes with my hands, only peeking out from between my fingers. Warmth washes over me, and then, with a suddenness that makes me jump, the book slams closed and the latch on its side lifts and locks itself.

There on the cover is stamped the double *W* emblem—one *W* gold, one silver. Now I understand what those *W*s mean. *Word Weaver.* Each *W* begins to glow, shooting gold and silver sparks into the air until the whole room is a fireworks display of gold and silver showers.

An apparition appears on the other side of the room, becoming clearer until I recognize it to be Gabrielle. She looks so beautiful, just as she had on that night I saw her dancing at the lawn party. But this time, the fear has vanished and Gabrielle's smile reaches her eyes. They sparkle as brightly as the gems on her dress. Gabrielle presses her fingers to her lips and blows me a kiss that rushes over to me like a gust of wind, swirling around me. This time the wind is warm with a hint of lilies, whispering a haunting "Thank you."

A young man joins her side and takes her hand. That must be the prince, I realize. He kisses her hand lightly and then the two begin dancing. They spin in circles, laughter filling the air.

Then the light from the book vanishes along with Gabrielle, and the room blankets to darkness. Wind swirls around me and it's as if the floor drops out from under me.

I plunge into an endless abyss so fast I don't even have time to scream.

* * *

I blink a few times and then lift my head, trying to figure out where I am and to make sense of everything that happened.

Then, as if by magic, Bella's face appears above me, a worried crease stretched across her brow. "Keira?" she says in a frantic tone. "Keira? Are you okay? Oh my gosh. Someone call an ambulance! Quick!"

My head jerks up. I throw my arms around Bella in the biggest hug ever.

"You're all right!" I say. "You got out of the tower?"

"Huh?" Bella says. "What tower?"

"You don't remember?"

"Girl," Bella says. "We were so worried about you! After the chandeliers crashed, Chet and I couldn't find you anywhere. And then we came out here, and you were passed out on the steps. I feel so awful. Will you forgive me?"

"What? I'm the one who should be apologizing."

"I should've listened to you about the ghost and how it was going to ruin the whole ball. I was so fixated on my designs that I didn't think about your safety. I promise not to be so selfish next time."

"Now you're being ridiculous. But why am I lying outside, on the top step of the castle stairs?"

A group of people on the grass are talking while Monsieur and the Joneses argue at the base of the stairs.

"We thought that ghost had finally got you," Chet says. "If you ask me, I think it was the ghost that made the chandeliers crash like that."

"Maybe it was just a bad dream." I rub the sides of my head.

Until a gleam of silver buried in the folds of my dress catches my eye. I lift my pen, cradling it in my hand.

Or maybe it wasn't a dream.

I think about the pen and the words I wrote. Maybe it's not the pen that is evil and nearly destroyed my family and best friend, but the words I chose to write. One thing I know: Words *are* powerful.

I tuck the pen back into my dress's sash and allow Bella to help me up.

"How's your dad, Chet?" I wobble on my feet, leaning hard against Bella. "I saw him pass out."

"He's feeling a little better now after he pretty much threw up all of his guts," Chet says. "I think he must have drank some of the Joneses' punch before we threw it out. I'm sure glad whatever stuff they put in there isn't lethal. Just make-you-really-sick kind of stuff. He's kind of ticked off right now.

"Oh! And is this yours?" Chet asks. He holds up a silver chalice, imprinted with the image of a ghost, hair flung behind her, skirts billowing out as if she were flying. "It was lying at your feet."

"Nope," I say, trying to steady the panic rising in me at seeing the ghost's chalice. "Looks like something from the gift shop."

"Yeah, you're probably right." Chet tosses it over his shoulder into the river. "Must be some trinket knockoff."

A siren fills the air along with flashing lights as four squad cars speed down the castle's dirt drive, spurting up a cloud of dust.

"About time the police showed up," Chet says.

The cars screech to a halt at the bottom of the stairs. Police jump out, holding Tasers and flashlights.

"You!" One police officer points at Bella, Chet, and me. "Don't move! Raise your hands!"

Instantly, we shoot our hands into the air, even though I can barely hold mine up since they're so weak from my castle climbing. Another person emerges from one of the squad cars. But it isn't a police officer, it's my mom!

"Don't shoot!" Mom screams. "That's my baby girl."

"Mom!" I shout. "You're here. Where have you been? Are you okay?"

Mom races up the stairs and draws me into a hug. "Oh, I'm perfectly fine. It's you I was worried about. I gave the police all of your evidence from your journal."

"My journal?" I cringe, expecting her to be mad that I'd been writing so much. "You took my journal and then showed it to other people?"

"It's hard-core evidence." Mom smiles warmly at me. "Good facts and solid evidence should never be ignored. You know, because you wrote all your observations, the police were able to follow some leads on the whole case. Perhaps writing isn't such a bad thing after all. I'm so proud of you, sweetie!"

Before long, the police have everyone escorted out of the castle, including the Joneses and Monsieur in handcuffs. Paramedics carefully ease Shan Valrose (aka Mr. Parker) onto a gurney and load him into the ambulance.

"I better go with my dad to the hospital," Chet tells me. "Maybe I'll see you again someday. You sure know how to make a boring holiday into a full-out adventure. Here's my email address if you're ever in Canada and want to go rock climbing."

"Sure." I take the piece of paper that Chet has scribbled his name and email address on. "Thanks for your help. The rock climbing sure came in handy."

Chet waves good-bye and jumps into the ambulance. A pang runs through me. I'm going to really miss him.

After I give my statement (of course leaving out the part about the ghost, my magic pen, and my fairy tale), I realize I haven't seen Madame or Ms. Teppernat since I came to on the castle stairs.

"Have you seen Madame and Ms. Teppernat?" I ask Bella.

"Who?" Bella says.

"You know, Madame DuPont, who runs this place, and Ms. Teppernat from *Girls' World*."

"I don't know who you're talking about," Bella says. "Renee is the one in charge here."

"And Cheryl Crooner is the coordinator for the magazine," Mom adds.

"I don't know what you did," Monsieur yells across the drive as an officer pushes him into the squad car. His hair, usually slicked back to perfection, rears up like a peacock, and his glasses are skewed on his face. "But I still think you are who I said you are. I may not be able to prove it now, but once I'm free, I'm going to find out the truth about all of this!"

Then the door slams in his face so he can't say another word. Through the car window, I can still see his mouth moving.

"That despicable man," Mom says. "I hope they find lots of reasons to keep him locked up."

"It's okay," I say. "Because I changed the fairy tale from an unhappy ending to happy. Now there's no way he can prove that a Word Weaver wrote it."

"Really!" Mom says, clearly shocked. "But how? I didn't think it was possible!"

"I'll tell you all about it later," I say. "But first I need to go check something."

I run back inside the castle with Mom and Bella close at my heels. I lead them past the butler, down the hall, and into the library. The château's history book is still lying on the desk where Chet left it. I flip through the pages until I find Gabrielle's story.

"Look!" I say. "Gabrielle no longer is murdered. She lives a happy life here in the castle! It really happened. I changed the ending!"

"I don't understand." Bella picks up my story from the magazine article that is also still on the desk from when Monsieur brought it to show me during our talk. "That's exactly how your story always ended."

Mom's eyebrows rise, and then she bursts out laughing. "So maybe you plagiarized a little. I can forgive that."

I join her laughing. Mom is a whole lot smarter, and funnier, than I ever realized.

"Do you think the story really happened?" I ask Mom. She nods, but I'm not satisfied with just that. "Bella, do you remember anything that happened in the ballroom tonight?"

"I remember you confronting the Joneses about spiking the punch!" Bella starts giggling. "That was epic."

"What about right after the chandeliers fell? When you were taken by the ghost?"

"Taken by a ghost?" Bella says, and now she's studying me closely as if she's worried I've gone insane.

"We don't remember any of that, sweetie," Mom says. Then, as we exit the library, Mom whispers into my ear, "Once a story happens, only the Word Weaver remembers all the versions of the story. The rest of us just take the final version as reality."

"I should never have written that awful story," I say.

"True." Mom squeezes me tighter. "But I should have trusted you and told you the whole truth. I was desperate to protect and shelter you, but it made everything worse. When we get home, we have a lot to talk about. No more secrets."

"No more secrets." I smile, a weight lifting off me. "That sounds like a really good plan."

"Which reminds me." Mom starts digging through her purse. "I think I have an article somewhere in here about the importance of not keeping secrets."

Bella and I groan.

"If all my stories ended up like this new version, maybe I should think about having a career in writing," I say.

Mom furrows her brows. "Now let's not get too crazy here."

I laugh at her expression but peek down at my magical pen clutched in the palm of my hand. It shimmers once, that bright sapphire blue. Winking.

Promising me a whole world of adventures.

THE END

From Princess to Princess

My love affair with the magical *Château de Chenonceau* began during a trip with my sister to France. Since both of us had careers as make-believe princesses, we had one destination in mind—the Loire Valley, the premiere location for enchanting castles. We toured castle after castle, but as the two of us strolled the wooded lane toward Chenonceau, instantly we knew this castle was special.

With my journal and pen in hand, we scoured every inch of the château. (Even sneaking into restricted places and tucking ourselves into fireplaces! Shhh! Don't tell!) We danced in the Gallery—which in *The Princess and the Page* I renamed the ballroom—and as we leaned over the balcony, we drank in the scent of lilies and gazed at the stunning gardens.

During our tour, I was captivated by the tragic story of Duchess Gabrielle d'Estrées. Born in 1573, she was raised in a castle in the town of Coeuvres where her strict father forced her to study rather than ride her beloved pony. Her mother abandoned the family when Gabrielle was ten, leaving her and her siblings to be raised by their aunt. In 1590, she met King Henry IV, and the two fell madly in love.

To show his love for Gabrielle, Henry IV acquired Chenonceau from Catherine de Médicis, although it was Gabrielle's son, César de Bourbon, who ended up with ownership. Today a bedroom is dedicated to Gabrielle, the very one that Keira stays in at the castle, and the ceiling of the Five Queens' bedroom is painted with the coat of arms of King Henry IV and Gabrielle.

When Henry passed on his coronation ring to Gabrielle in March of 1599, she was thrilled knowing that the two of them were finally to be married. But heartbreakingly, on April 10, 1599, she became suddenly ill and died at the age of twenty-six.

King Henry IV was devastated, especially when word spread that she probably had been poisoned. Loving her even in death, he gave Gabrielle the funeral of a queen and wore black, the first French monarch to wear black for mourning.

Moved by this tragic love story, I perched on the railing of Chenonceau's bridge and began to write in my journal. But as I stared down at my pen, a new thought occurred to me. *What if a special pen could rewrite the story so that Gabrielle and Henry could have their happily ever after? What if a pen, like the one I was holding, had magical powers?*

And so, I fictionalized Gabrielle's story, blending some of the facts of her life with my own make-believe narrative, which became Keira's tale.

My writer juices started flowing and the inspiration for *The Princess and the Page* was born. Still, the idea of "happily ever after" irked me because sometimes in real life, it seems like those endings don't exist. I brought those feelings into Keira's story. She makes good and bad decisions, but with each of those she holds the power to begin her "once upon a time" and create her own "happily ever after."

Keira's story is about living out our lives and making the best of every situation by finding the beauty and love even in our Dark Towers of life.

Today, as I wish upon a star, I hope you will never stop believing that you have the power to bring magic to the world around you.

With love,
Christina

Glossary

aucun — none

allez — come on

au revoir — good-bye

bon — good

bonjour — hello

bon appétit — good appetite

château — castle

entrecôte — rib-eye steak

délicieux — delicious

Dimanche — Sunday

Jeudi — Thursday

la nuit de la mort — night of death

Vendredi — Friday

Lundi — Monday

mademoiselle — miss

manuel de l'immobilier — handbook of real estate

Mardi — Tuesday

merci — thank you

Mercredi — Wednesday

monsieur — gentleman

non — no

nous devons parler — we have to talk

oh là là — oh my

oui — yes

pétanque — a game where one stands inside a circle and throws a metal ball as close as possible to a smaller wooden ball

pain perdu — French toast

profiteroles au chocolat — cream puff with chocolate

voilà — there it is or there you have it

Acknowledgments

Thank you, God, for your blessings. You amaze me.

I am incredibly appreciative to my readers who have read my stories and are an inspiration to me. To the educators, librarians, and bloggers across the world who have been an amazing support. I love how stories have brought us together!

To Isabella Pagani for allowing me to use your beautiful name.

When I first saw the cover for *The Princess and the Page*, there were tears in my eyes because it was that perfect. So thank you to Petur Antonsson for creating such an enchanting cover.

I am indebted to Jillian Nightingale and Ken McNeilly for their expertise and advice on the French language. Any mistakes in this beautiful language are mine.

Thank you to my agent, Jeff Ourvan, for his insights into this story and tirelessly believing in my writing.

This book wouldn't have come to life without my inspirational editor, Andrea Pinkney, who is a Word Weaver and princess in every way. When she called to talk about *The Princess and the Page*, I knew Keira's story had found the perfect home. I'm also incredibly grateful to the whole Scholastic team who are busy weaving magic this very moment. To my copyeditor, Joy Simpkins, and designer, Carol Ly: Your work and efforts are so appreciated!

Special hugs to my fellow Word Weavers who literally dropped everything for emergency reads and my bizarre questions: Debbie Ridpath Ohi, Beth Revis, Andrea Mack, Carmella VanVleet, and Susan Laidlaw. These ladies are truly magical!

To my Seoul Foreign writer's group, the Inkwells, for their critiques: Dale Wood, Afaf Finan, Brent Van Staalduinen, Lonna Lutze Hill, and Doug Farley. Also, a big thanks to Jeff Bolinger, Shelley Jewell, and Mary Gibson, who graciously read an early version of this book.

Writing can be a solitary art, which is why I'm thankful to my fellow princesses in crime: Vivi Barnes, Amy Christine Parker, and Lynne Matson, who always put up with my crazy ideas. Road trip in tiaras!

As always, my family has been with me on this journey the whole way. Thanks Dad, Mom, David, and Cassia. And especially to Julianne for encouraging me to write my princess story. Oh the fun we had sneaking through Château de Chenonceau, drinking cafés, and eating chocolate croissants!

To my boys, Caleb and Luke, who are my everything: Long after the pages of this book have turned to dust, my love will still be there.

And to Doug, my love and prince: I love you, I love you, I love you! I pull out my Word Weaver pen and write, *And they lived happily ever after.*

About the Author

CHRISTINA FARLEY is the author of the bestselling Gilded series. Prior to that, she worked as an international teacher and at a top secret job for Disney, where she was known to scatter pixie dust before the sun rose. When not traveling the world or creating imaginary ones, she spends time with her husband and two sons in Clermont, Florida, where they are busy preparing for the next World Cup, baking cheesecakes, and raising a pet dragon that's in disguise as a cockatiel. You can visit her online at www.ChristinaFarley.com.